Totally Bound Publishing books by Lupa Garneau:

Children of Shairobi
Primal Desire

I0542366

Children of Shairobi

PRIMAL DESIRE

LUPA GARNEAU

Primal Desire
ISBN # 978-1-78430-320-4
©Copyright Lupa Garneau
Cover Art by Posh Gosh ©Copyright October 2014
Interior text design by Claire Siemaszkiewicz
Totally Bound Publishing

Published in 2014 by Totally Bound Publishing, Newland House, The Point, Weaver Road, Lincoln, LN6 3QN, United Kingdom.

Totally Bound Publishing is a subsidiary of Totally Entwined Group Limited.

PRIMAL DESIRE

Dedication

For my own Mother Goddess.

Chapter One

Nexhan sniffed the air, his nostrils flaring as he tested the scents — the crispness of the weeds, the softness of the wild flowers in full bloom and the sweetness of the sequoia sap. He flicked his ears and looked up. The trees filled overhead, their thin leaves making way for only a few ribbons of sunlight to stream down, lighting up the fog like clouds of silver.

Home.

It had been too long since he had looked upon the giants of the forest, the forever living, and he couldn't help the surge of warmth that spread through him. Here was the raw, primal beauty of the Mother, the majesty of life and perseverance, and Nexhan had almost forgotten why he had left in the first place.

He reared up on his powerful hind legs and unsheathed his claws, the curved weapons sinking into the twelve-inch thick bark. He pulled, feeling his claws stretch and the bark give away into tiny splinters. He knew this tree, remembered when it had been a ten-foot sapling. That had been over seven hundred years ago.

His sensitive ears caught the smooth cooing of a hawk in the distance and he craned his neck, watching a branch shift above him. The low caterwaul of a bobcat sounded far away. He curled his lips back and issued a roar, a reclaiming shout that stretched across the land and echoed through the trees. It was his declaration of returning, his staking of the territory, and a stern reminder to all that dwell here that the boss was back on duty.

He was home.

Nexhan fell back on all fours, the cool dirt shifting under the pads of his heavy paws. The grasses and wood debris tickled his toes as he pulled his massive weight forward, inhaling the calming scent of the forest. It was so welcomed against the overwhelming stink of the human city — all that rotting garbage and pollutants. He wondered how he had ever survived living in the metal forests of humanity.

He arched his back and rubbed himself against the scratchy bark of a Sitka spruce, spreading his scent along the surface. Like many of the trees, their trunks were covered in mats of moss, the tiny, sage-green bristles soft against his pelt like thousands of little fingers.

He cocked his head and perked his ears as the soft beat of wings caught his attention. He knew this sound, and despite having been away for so long, he recognized it instantly. A hummingbird emerged from the shrub, the steady pumping of its little wings like a blur of color as it hovered in front of him. The creature's thread-thin beak poked him gently in the nose, the bird's body no bigger than his nostril. He chuffed a hello, his breath sending the bird backward, and the tiny thing floated away into the bushes to do its business.

Nexhan took a deep breath and stuck his tongue out, tasting the scents, reacquainting himself with the forest. A cool breeze swept down and flowed through the trees, rattling their branches softly. It caressed his fur like a parent's reassuring touch and he reveled in the contact, his heart soaring.

The song of earth was all about him. It was in every tree, every root, every stone. It was in the air, in the tiny spores and pollen grains that danced in the wild winds. It was in the hummingbirds, the hawks and the insects. It reached out through the moss and the ferns, and shot up through the giant sequoias, spreading out into the sky, churning with the mighty thunderheads. It was energy, *life*. He was being welcomed home by the forest, the beasts and the birds, and by his Mother. It felt wonderful. There were no words to describe her melodies, her gentle hums and deep crescendos. Beauty was too plain a word.

Along with the breeze came a peculiar scent. He curled his lips over his fangs and sucked in so that he could get a better taste. It wasn't one of his brothers, but it wasn't wholly animal, either. Curious, he padded over the lush forest floor, silent as a snake, and made his way toward the scent. It was fresh, earthy, with the spice of male musk.

He weaved through the huge trunks and padded softly over the brush, his paws making not a sound as he closed in on the intruder. Nexhan lowered his head and flattened his ears as he drew closer, the sound of thumping and agitated growls filling the air. The creature was making so much noise that he was likely to pass as a human, as clumsy and loud as *they* were. And humans frequented this forest. Mostly tourists. They called Nexhan's home Redwood National Park, but to him it was *Weywoni Le Gai*, home to the red daughters, the ever living of the Mother.

Nexhan peered out from behind a sequoia, his nostrils flaring wider this time as he observed the cougar—a young male, sleek and muscular—darting around, pouncing as if he were playing tag with a swift-footed rabbit. He was in good health, his body strong, beautifully built—made to kill and protect—but his movements were awkward and uncoordinated. His coat was smooth and tawny, his eyes a most peculiar violet like the twilight sky, and he had an air of youthful uncertainty about him.

He was shifter, just like Nexhan. But, what was he doing here?

Nexhan cocked his head in intrigue and stepped out, making himself known. This was Rune Fang territory, and although wild cougars made this forest their home, the cougar-shifters very rarely strayed into his domain. They tended to keep to the mountain regions, scouring the cliffs of the Rockies and building their homes around the high-altitude forests.

The cat jerked when Nexhan chuffed a greeting, the male's body stiffening, ears flattening. He hissed a warning but fear lurked his eyes. Not fear as though he believed he'd be harmed, but fear of the unknown. Nexhan understood. His species was on the brink of extinction and a young cougar-shifter wouldn't recognize a Rune Fang if one pounced him head on.

Nexhan chuffed again, attempting to ease the male's uncertainty. He stopped a few feet from the smaller cat and eyed him with amusement. The male curled into himself, his hackles up, claws unsheathed, those lovely eyes watching him with wariness.

Using the current of energy that flowed out from the earth and known only to shifters and their ilk, he plucked a thread and relayed the message, *"You're a long way from home. Why are you on Rune Fang land?"*

The male seemed stunned as his mind filled with Nexhan's words. Perhaps he hadn't been taught how to communicate using the language of the earth? Well, he was young, but all cubs were shown how to read the currents, decipher them and send their own thoughts through. But the cougar-shifter merely blinked at Nexhan, his ears going back, his pupils expanding as though he were deep in concentration.

Nexhan tried again, *"What is your name?"*

The male didn't respond, just pushed his butt back against a rock and hissed. Nexhan towered over him, his height twice that of the young male, his weight nearly triple, and the cougar-shifter was spitting at *him*? Really? A bit annoyed and maybe a little amused, Nexhan curled his lip, letting the cat get a good look at the fourteen-inch fangs protruding from his skull—as though they could be missed with a closed maw, anyway? For laughs, he roared an ear-piercing shout of superiority.

The cougar-shifter started, his pupils dilating further, his ears flattening so much that he looked goofy, but he made no move to run. He wouldn't. That would be a show of weakness, and young males were notorious for their foolish bravery. The humans called it balls of steel. Either way, the cat wasn't backing down, even when he knew he had no chance of besting the six-foot Rune Fang in front of him.

Nexhan considered roughing up the cougar a bit, show him one didn't disrespect a clan leader in his own territory, but a familiar call caught his attention. He perked his ears and didn't miss the way the cougar relaxed. Nexhan answered the call with an inviting roar, the mighty rumble shaking the very earth.

The male wasn't too far off, a quarter of a mile if Nexhan had judged the distance correctly. His brother responded again, a sound of eager anticipation. Nexhan wondered how the clan would welcome him back. Would they be angry that he had abandoned them or happy that he had returned to his family? He wasn't sure, but the call of the fellow Rune Fang was music to his ears, as sweet as the voice of the Mother herself.

Nexhan settled his gaze on the young cougar-shifter and whipped his tail back and forth playfully. The ancestors of the big cats, the Saber-Toothed Tigers had had short, stubby tails, but Rune Fangs possessed long, flowing appendages tipped with colorful fur that was used in a variety of expressions. Though, most Rune Fangs took offense to being grouped with the extinct cats. While all livings things were born of the Mother, the Children of Shairobi were divine in their own right, the result of the union between two gods.

The cougar-shifter watched warily, but seemed to have relaxed, his ears coming up in attention. He was peculiar no doubt, and Nexhan was curious to see his human form. It was hard to judge exactly just how old he was, but Nexhan reckoned early twenties, not necessarily a cub.

His brother's chuffing pulled his attention away from the cougar-shifter and he chuffed back at the large male padding his way over. His sable-colored coat was smooth and shiny. Darker stripes of auburn streamed across his face and back in thick bands growing thinner the further they went. His large chest puffed with heavy breath, the neck and underbelly paling into cream, and one of his fangs was broken at the tip. His orange-tipped tail shimmied back and forth in excitement, and his dark yellow eyes, rimmed in orange—the color of a sunset—were wide in disbelief.

Nexhan instantly recognized his clan brother. *"Nakoda?"*

The male chuffed louder, the waves of communication hitting Nexhan like a brick wall of excitement. *"Nexhan? You've returned?"*

If he could smile as a cat, he would. *"Yes, brother. It is I!"*

Suddenly, the male set into motion, his big body crashing up against Nexhan. They banged heads, and Nakoda whipped his tail, moaning as he curled his weight around Nexhan. Nexhan soared inside, his heart banging against his ribcage, and he swore he could have grown wings and taken to the sky. His clan brother! His closest friend!

Nakoda flattened his ears and growled, batting Nexhan in the face with his tail playfully. *"I thought a mockingbird-shifter was playing a joke on me. Surely, I never expected the call of my clan leader to fill this forest once more."*

Nexhan laughed inside. Of course there was no such thing as a mockingbird-shifter, but there were those that could become huge raptors, birds of prey such as hawks and eagles that tended to be skilled vocally. *"And I would say I'm nothing more than an illusion. But, I am here."*

He was aware of the cougar-shifter watching them intently, fascination crossing the cat's face as he tried to catch the waves flowing back and forth. The cougar seemed as though he wanted to join in on the show of affection, but he stayed put, his butt planted firmly on the forest floor.

Nakoda followed Nexhan's interest and flicked his ears. *"His name is Colban."* When the cougar hissed,

Nakoda corrected, *"Cole… I've been trying to show him how to speak through the earth, but so far he's only been able to receive messages, not send them."*

Realizing they were talking about him, the cougar-shifter squeaked a greeting, the coo very much sounding like a hello. It was just a simple trick of shifting his vocal cords, much like the 'I love you' dog Nexhan had seen in a website video the humans called YouTube.

Nexhan chuffed in greeting then blinked at his friend. *"Is he lost?"*

"Cole has been with us for three months now," Nakoda said then turned to regard the young male. He growled low in his throat. *"Go back to the village and let the clan know our leader has returned."*

Cole cocked his head and curled his tail around his paws, apparently in confusion. His glowing violet eyes were attentive, interested, but his body had grown lax, the uncertainty melting away into curious content. Then he looked at Nexhan with awe and…intrigue?

"Quickly now," Nakoda growled.

The cocky male turned his back to them and whisked his tail high in the air, letting them get a good look at his jewels, a motion of disregard for authority. He quickly disappeared behind the trees before Nakoda could reprimand his impudence.

Nakoda shook his head as if he were trying to rid himself of an annoying insect. *"Young males. Their egos transcend the species."*

"You're going to complain? We were much the same way, if you haven't forgotten, old man," Nexhan teased, shoving his weight up against the other cat in a playful push.

"If I recall correctly, you were the instigator and I was the one who always had to get you out of trouble," Nakoda chided, his eyes bright with amusement. *"And who are you calling old? We were born the same year."*

"Yes, but I'm two months younger," Nexhan quipped. He sniffed the air, wondering if any of his other brothers were in the vicinity.

Nakoda was quiet for a few moments, his face thoughtful, amber eyes tracking Nexhan's every movement. He let out a big breath. *"We've missed you. Nashuk has tried several times to form a search party. Everyone practically agreed someone needed to track you down, but no one was willing to go."*

"No one is angry with me for leaving?" Nexhan asked incredulously. Of course, they wouldn't have come for him. Before he'd left, he had explicitly forbade any to come after him, and many were anxious about entering large human establishments. He didn't blame them. Leaving one's home wasn't easy and it had been torture for him.

Nakoda growled and pounced on Nexhan, who was caught off guard. His friend's weight pushed him to the ground. He laughed inside, rolling over on his back as the male bit him playfully on the neck, his thick fur absorbing the deadly fangs. He clawed the cat's hide gently in acceptance.

"Are you kidding? You are our clan leader," Nakoda said sternly. *"And more importantly, our brother. Of course we're happy you're back."*

Nexhan sighed then wiggled out of Nakoda's grasp and walked away in silence, stopping to look up at the reaching sequoias. They were so tall, so proud and strong. It was a little known fact that their roots were shallow, the dozens of fingers that anchored their impossibly tall bodies running close to the surface. But they spread out far and wide, linking with the surrounding trees and creating a network of support for themselves and other trees. They established a unity with one another, a community where each was as important as the other and, if one fell, it left a vulnerability in the network. That tight-knit structure has allowed them to survive for thousands of years, the strength of each other keeping them stout against the vicious winds.

The Rune Fang clan was much the same way.

Nexhan sighed and whispered along the waves, *"It takes more than blood to make a clan leader. I'm a coward for abandoning the family."*

And he was, no matter how much his friend was willing to argue the point. The Rune Fang were on the verge of extinction, numbering only fourteen at the time of his departure one-hundred years ago. While most shifters were endangered, his people were hanging by a thread. It was only a matter of time before the great guardian cats of Shairobi disappeared forever. They had no more females to breed with, and the males that had tried to mate with human women over the centuries were met mostly with failure. They could live forever—if circumstance allowed it—but they were not immortal. All it took to end their existence was a well-placed blade.

How had it come to this? His people had once been a great tribe. They had been the guardians that watched over the portals the gods used to travel between worlds. They were the strongest, the fiercest of the earth-shifters, and part of the savage warriors of the Mother, battling her enemies with pride and bravery. The humans called the beasts they resembled saber-toothed tigers, but they were the Gatekeepers to those who remembered the old days.

Now they were nothing more than a memory, a story told to cubs around a campfire like a fairytale.

Nexhan knew why he had left. The memory came back to him like a floating wisp of smoke. He had been afraid his brothers would have seen the weakness that had dug its claw into his heart and soul. Once he had been in impenetrable mountain, but he had quickly been reduced to rubble within a few hours. The hurt had been etched upon his face as surely as the stripes graced his fur. He had been terrified of failing them as both a leader and a Rune Fang. And then there was the anger, the insatiable need for revenge.

So he had run—run from all that he had known in thirst for justice against who that had wronged him so irrevocably.

"Heartbreak is nothing to be ashamed of, Nexhan," the male said softly.

"I was clan leader. I should have acted as one," he refuted.

Nakoda huffed and bumped his body up against Nexhan. *"You still are. Now come. I'm sure everyone is anxious to greet their brother."*

Nexhan made a sound of acknowledgment and reluctantly followed his friend. He'd admit he was excited about seeing his home again, dying to feel his clan's emotions as his own. He was afraid that he'd been away too long—that he'd forgotten what it was like to be one with the Mother and all her creatures—but as he followed Nakoda, he felt that link slowly returning.

Making light conversation, Nakoda said, *"The village is thriving. It's become a waypoint for traveling shifters. Cougars and raptors frequent the village as well as the occasional bear."*

17

Nexhan digested that news then inquired, *"This is where Cole comes in?"*

His friend's chuckle entered Nexhan's mind. *"Yes and no. Cole is a bit of mystery. He came to us as a scared, defensive little thing. He's mellowed out a bit, but I don't think he knows who he is."*

Nexhan turned that over in his head for a bit.

"Butch visited us several years ago and helped us install solar panels that allow us to use electrical devices. It is quite amazing. Travelers often bestow us with mechanical gifts, and we have amassed quite a collection. Much of the clan was fearful at first, but I think everyone has seen the usefulness of such machines," Nakoda explained. *"Did you know that you can speak to someone in real time halfway across the globe?"*

"I do. Had I known the village had access to phones, I would have..." Nexhan sighed, unable to finish.

Nakoda didn't respond. They walked back to the village in silence. The sequoias thinned out, growing shorter and younger, the width of their trunks smaller. The foliage and ferns thinned out as well, the grasses newer and the air less thick with trace amounts of pollen.

Nexhan stopped and shivered, a low hum running through his body. He had felt the gentle vibrations earlier in the day, but now they were becoming an uncomfortable quake deep in his body. It wasn't cold—the midsummer air, mild and welcoming, combined with the fluff of his fur—but he had been in this form for several days. Although it felt as natural as breathing, his existence as shifter demanded balance between his animal and human halves.

Shifters were neither human nor animal, but both—a heart and a soul intertwined and forever living, creating a union. But they had to keep a balance between their two halves. Most stayed human during the day and would shift at night, roaming the forests only to fall asleep in the sweet embrace of the Mother.

Nakoda asked, *"Been in form long?"*

"Several days. I shifted once I got close to the forest. I slept and hunted as such, as well," he said, looking into the face of his friend.

"How did you ever survive staying human while in the city?" The male shivered.

Nexhan chuckled. *"With a lot of determination. A tiger I bumped into showed me how to alter my form to that of a household cat. It got uncomfortable quite quickly, though. But if the desire to shift got too great, I'd head to the forests. You don't know how many times I wanted to keep running and not stop until I felt the soil of* Weywoni Le Gai *under my paws again."*

The male digested that news for a few seconds before sending along waves of approval. *"Well, don't let me stop you."*

Nexhan relaxed and let the hum grow outward, the vibrations traveling along his spine and encompassing every fiber of his being. Changing wasn't exactly easy, especially when he would have to hold back the natural shifting and upset the delicate balance of his existence. But the uncomfortable currents quickly morphed into a soft caress and before he knew it, he was standing on flat feet, his spine erect, his skin exposed to the gentle caress of the wind and the cooler temperature. Nexhan blinked and ran his hand through his long, dark blue locks.

"Better?" Nakoda curled his lip in a toothy smile.

Nexhan smiled back. "Yeah. Better."

Nexhan watched as his brother shivered, his own shift rising up. Describing the change was hard to do. There were very few words in the language of humans that could detail the emotions, the splitting of the two bodies and the reforming of the soul. But the great cat disintegrated into a bright, colorful light, the illumination reshaping from that of a quadruped cat to one of a bipedal human.

Stretching his naked, lightly sun-darkened body, Nakoda grinned becomingly. He was handsome, always had been with that dark orange hair framing a sharp, regal face and high cheekbones. Their human hair always matched the shade of their tails. His lips were quirked up in a friendly gesture, his amber eyes shining with happiness. He had blue runes painted on his body, notably on his chest and thighs. It was common for Rune Fangs to ward their bodies. It helped protect them against the eyes of humans. If one human got a look at a giant cat with oversized fangs that was supposed to be extinct, then the forest would be swarming with Nessie and Bigfoot hunters looking for the next big thing. This way, with the wards working their magic, a human wouldn't really be sure what they were seeing, if they even saw anything at all. It was how they had survived as humans encroached on their territory.

Nexhan cocked a brow. "Have you been running around all night and day? You're buff."

The male chuckled and rolled his massive shoulders. "Something like that."

Nexhan grinned softly, taking a deep breath and inhaling the varying scents of the forest. Goddess, it felt so good to be home. The earth was cool and soft under his bare feet, his skin fully exposed to the embrace of the breeze. This was life in all its purest majesty.

"Shall we?" Nakoda held his hand out.

Nexhan nodded. "We shall."

They walked side by side, Nakoda bumping his arm up against Nexhan's in a gentle show of affection. The thick trees broke and a clearing came into view. The field was heavy with spring grass, wild flowers of blue, yellow and white dotting the turf. It was a good-sized clearing with the village in the center. Fields green with the growth of crops surrounded the cabins as well as all stalks of corn, stretching vines of pumpkin and squash, rows and rows of tomatoes and strawberries. The fruit-baring trees stood watch behind the crop fields, their branches not yet heavy with the weight of apples, pears and peaches. Wait, were those palm trees?

"We had a trio of traveling Jaguars pass by a few years ago. They gifted us with the seeds of banana and coconut trees. Of course we had to enchant the air around the trees, else they'd die during the cooler months," Nakoda explained. "But every year, we are blessed to enjoy the fruits of the tropics."

To the side of the fields stood the barn where the clan raised cows for milk and chickens for eggs. There were a couple dozen small cabins in rows encircling the main two-story lodge, where the clan held council and dined together, but what really held one's attention was the giant sequoia centered in the middle of the settlement. It grew tall, over four hundred feet, its base nearly thirty feet wide. It was the only tree for a mile, but it was not like the others.

The Rune Fangs called it *Weynka Le Gai*, first daughter of the Mother. It had been planted when they had arrived from Shairobi over thirty-thousand years ago. Though it was a solitary tree, unlike the other redwoods, its roots went deep, digging into the soil and cutting through the rocks to unite with the core of the earth. The raw energy of the planet flowed up through its roots. It was the source of their magic, the energies in which they used to transcribe their wards and protect their home.

Tears pricked Nexhan's eyes. He felt the hum of the wards as they crossed into the clearing. Their home had been protected from the prying eyes of humans for centuries, the same spells that they used on their bodies kept the village invisible and allowed only those with shifter blood to enter. It was how they had remained hidden all these years while humanity took over the earth and cut down the forests.

Nexhan craned his neck as he spotted the cougar-shifter watching him from the edge of the clearing, his body lax, his eyes shining with interest and his tawny coat gleaming in the sunlight. The male shook his head then moseyed off into the forest, flicking his tail cockily one last time.

A shout went up, catching Nexhan's attention, and he watched as the village came alive with activity. His clan brothers. He took a deep breath, beating back the shame of abandoning his family, and prodded through the wild grass, his pace picking up as males began bursting out of cottages.

"Told you so," Nakoda muttered playfully.

He couldn't help but to smile as the clan link began to hum through his body as surely as if he'd been hit by a lightning bolt. It felt wonderful. It made him feel alive again, the connectedness awaking every cell of his being. His brothers rushed to him and he met them halfway, several strong males crashing into him. Shouts rang in his ears. Their big bodies embraced him, hugged him, pulling him close, their skins sliding against one another. The link zipped through him, their emotions swirling around him. Joy. Love. It was almost too much for him to handle.

"Tonight we shall feast!" Hihano, a light-skinned, blond-haired male thrust a fist into the air and shouted.

Nexhan couldn't help but laugh as he was led into the village, immense excitement flying through his body. Neither Nakoda, nor anyone else, asked if he had sated his appetite for revenge, and he was glad for that. It didn't matter to them.

Only one thing did.

I am home.

* * * *

Cole watched the big male enter the clearing, his human body broad and lightly tanned. He was extremely muscular but then again, so were all Rune Fangs, their frames easily reaching seven feet, their weight exceeding two hundred and fifty pounds of pure power. Long, dark blue hair flowed over his shoulders and down his back like a wild river under the night sky, the locks appearing incredibly smooth and shiny. He'd bet they were as soft as flower petals.

The guy had a fine ass too.

Cole sniffed the air, attempting to pick up the Rune Fang's scent, but he was upwind. Shifter scents tended to have a basis of similarity regardless of shape, but he wanted to inhale that dark spice again. It was like chocolate to the nose.

Nexhan. That was his name. It was a signature he had heard often whispered amongst the Rune Fangs in the few months he'd lived here—a name afforded great respect and admiration—and the male certainly lived up to the hype. Both Nexhan's cat and human forms would easily frighten even the biggest, bravest cougar-shifter. His cat had been a thing of great

23

beauty and fierce strength. His coat was dark, a deep sepia, his stripes thick and black, and the bands spanned his entire back. His entire tail had been the color of the midnight sky from base to tip, and the long, flowing fur at the edge had wavered in the breeze like a flag, declaring his dominance. And those eyes...two glowing yellow moons outlined in dark orange just peeking over the horizon. They had been piercing, penetrating... They made Cole quake in his paws.

The only good thing about living here among the Rune Fangs was the eye candy and Nexhan was the Burdick to their Hershey's. *Mmm...*

Cole had been a fool in front of the clan leader, though. He hadn't even realized the male had been watching him until he heard the telltale chuffing of a Rune Fang. He'd never seen that particular cat before and he knew well they were few. He hadn't been afraid of being harmed, but he had been embarrassed by the show of his lack of skills. Surely Nexhan thought him nothing more than an overgrown cub.

Cole sighed when Nexhan gazed in his direction. Completely abashed, Cole padded off into the forest, seeking the solitude of the trees. He walked slowly, feeling the way the soil absorbed his weight, liking the way the sword ferns brushed up against his hide. He plopped to the ground and rolled on to his back, staring up into the thick boughs of the sequoias. He could barely see the blue of the sky, the silver fog embracing the trees like thick blankets.

He really liked it here. It was so beautiful.

Birds chirped softly in the trees. An owl screeched. He didn't need to see the sun to know it was slinking toward the west, falling into the deep blue of the ocean. The nocturnal beasts would be rising soon, ready to begin the night. He licked his chops hungrily. He hadn't eaten since early morning and shifters could easily put away five-thousand calories a day. After all, they ate for two. The red-haired Rune Fang Nakoda, had been trying to show him how to hunt properly, but when Cole failed epically, the male would wander off in frustration.

Cole didn't blame him. He knew he was a sorry excuse for a shifter. It was embarrassing and part of the reason he had left his home. Feeling sorry for himself, he had tried to perfect his pouncing techniques where no one could see his clumsy movements, and look how that had turned out.

Nexhan, the clan leader of the Rune Fang—of all people—had watched with amusement as Cole shamed himself. Cole had heard the stories, the legends the elder Earth-Touched told around the fires. The mighty Rune Fang, the Gatekeepers, the Mother Goddess's chosen, battling her enemies with fierce determination. Hell, he had thought them nothing more than fables until Nakoda had found him a few months back.

Cole blinked, rubbing his head over some redwood sorrel that resembled three-leaf clovers. He sneezed and covered his face with a big paw. He didn't feel like returning to the village and just wanted to lay here all night, alone in his miseries. He was such a failure—and his parents wanted him to mate an Earth-Touched female? What had gotten into their heads with that bright idea? He could barely care for himself, so how was he expected to care for a woman and possible cubs? And hell, he was only twenty-seven. He wasn't ready to settle down and raise a family.

Cole would be the first to admit the female had been beautiful. She was a few years older than him but not many. She had long, wheat-blonde hair and sparkling sky-blue eyes, as was common among cougar-shifters. Her features were soft, her skin a creamy tan, close to her cat form. She was a little shorter than he was but she was beautifully made with full breasts and a nice, rounded ass—a fine mate for any male. The thing that really scared him, though, was the fact that she was Earth-Touched. Many females were, but not all. Earth-Touched was a title given to those blessed with the sight of the Mother. They could interpret the subtle signs of the earth so that the clans could prepare for earthquakes, droughts and various other natural disasters. The Earth-Touched would bless the new pregnancies and births, lead the ceremonies of equinoxes and other holidays. They were sacred, special and…

He was supposed to mate one? Yeah, right. He was a shitty excuse for a mate. She deserved better. If it hadn't been for his lineage, he wouldn't have even been considered. The Nicoyla line stretched back thousands of years, his ancestors some of the first cougar-shifters to roam these lands. His intended mate had come from a similar line, and his parents said the union would strengthen their blood.

That and… Well, he had tried to be what she needed and as beautiful as she was, she wasn't for him. He had known that right away. That was another reason why he had left. The pressure to mate someone he didn't love—a creature he wasn't attracted to and could never be—was too much, so he had fled, traveling for days until entering the forests of the red daughters where Nakoda had found him half-starved and weary. He had been en route to a city called Los Angeles, but he had been too tired to continue on.

Cole had been thankful for the Rune Fangs' kindness. They had kept him well fed and provided the lowest level of companionship he allowed them to give. He'd tended to the animals, milked the cows, collected eggs and helped in the field, but the clan had learned right away not to ask him on hunts. Or fishing. The first time Nakoda had tried to show him how to throw a net, he had slipped and fallen into the water. *Idiot*.

Goddess, what was wrong with him? Was he just a natural klutz or was he flawed somehow? Even when his father had taken him out, tried to show him the right way to prowl, to kill, Cole had fucked it up. He hated disappointing the male, could see the frustration in his father's eyes. His dad was a fierce cougar, a successful hunter and a long-standing protector of the clan. How was he supposed to live up to that? Hell, he couldn't even communicate properly. Every time he tried to relay his thoughts along the energy currents, they ended up shooting in random directions, as if he had attached his words to a slingshot and aimed blindly. He felt castrated, less of a man. The males provided for the clan, hunted, protected the cubs and females. He could hardly provide for himself.

Well, that didn't matter as much as it should, because he had no desire to mate a female. He liked males too much, liked all that hard strength, that domineering personality. Homosexuality wasn't frowned upon in the clans. Hell, it didn't even have a title, it just *was*. Shifters viewed the union of two mates as the joining of two souls, two hearts. Male and female, male and male, or female and female, it didn't matter. That was all fine and dandy except he felt as though he'd disappoint his parents further if he didn't mate the Earth-Touched female then breed.

Her name was Bessa, a word that meant gentle one. He had talked to her quite a bit and they had gone for long walks in the forests. He even enjoyed their conversations. She smiled so sweetly at him and appeared to be into him. And when she had kissed him in the shadow of a huge evergreen, he'd balked. He couldn't do it, couldn't tie himself and her to a loveless mating where she would be left wondering why her lover didn't find her attractive. She was, but not to him—not in that way. So he had run until his paws were ready to fall off.

Cole sighed and rolled onto his side. He'd been here three months, but it seemed longer than that. Time was funny that way. The Rune Fangs had sent his parents a message via air to let them know that he needed time before he tied himself to a female. They had accepted, and the mating had been pushed back. But how long before he confessed the truth and watched the disappointment cross their faces?

He growled at himself and tried to force the emotions from his mind. Maybe he could just stay here for a while then head to the city as he had planned. Wasn't that what Nexhan had done? He heard the Rune Fangs talk about going to the city to find their clan leader, the separation wearing on their souls.

Nexhan... Cole knew he needed to stop the fantasies running through his head. The male was handsome, potent. Cole imagined being taken by him, that immense strength embracing him, that big body sliding up against his. Most shifter males tended to be dominant, but Cole wanted to submit to the power that was Nexhan.

He shivered inside and covered his face with his paw. He needed to get that idea out of his head. Males like Nexhan didn't lean toward a loser like him—at least he didn't think so, but he was making that judgment from his experiences among humanity, which was wider than his experience with his own kind. Sad, really. But he had always felt as though something wasn't quite right with him and he'd withdrawn into the world of humanity.

Cole wasn't sure how long he'd lain there. The birds were chattering away, singing their songs, waving good-bye to the sun. The fog had lifted a little and the first of the nocturnal creatures were beginning to stir. He wasn't far from the village, so he easily caught the scent of cooking food.

The Rune Fangs would feast tonight. He wanted to be there, wanted to observe the light-hearted cheer and see Nexhan again, but he knew that would be a bad idea. Hell, he wasn't sure if he was embarrassed having been watched or too afraid to initiate a conversation with the big male because he was attracted to him.

What did it matter, though?

Cole got to his feet, planted his rump on the forest carpet and looked up at the light fog swirling around the trees. The crickets had just begun to sing, their chorus of chirps loud to his ears. He watched an owl soar through the branches. His ears caught the rustling of ferns as something big moved behind him. It was probably a bear drawn in by the scent of food. The air shifted and he scented the unique musk. Fresh rain and danger, like a building thunderstorm.

Storm blinked at him from behind cold, silver eyes. The male was huge, his coat dark gray on the top, slowly bleeding into a deep cerulean blue the lower it went. Instead of stripes, spots marbled his hide and silver tipped his tail, reminding Cole of lightning. He looked more like an oversized leopard with sabers than a Rune Fang. Cole had only seen the big cat a few times, the male preferring to remain elusive.

Why, Cole wasn't sure.

Storm penetrated Cole with those ice-chip eyes, almost as if he were looking into his soul. Then, as quickly as he had appeared, he strutted past Cole and disappeared into the dense trees. He must have heard Nexhan's roar earlier and was going back to celebrate the return of his clan leader. Cole had heard the proclaiming roar, but he hadn't thought anything of it. He had assumed it was one of the Rune Fangs. He had only been with them a short while and it was difficult to distinguish their calls from one another.

Cole growled softly as his stomach reminded him it was time to eat, the alluring scent of roasting meat not helping his appetite. He feared the looks of disappointment Nexhan might show him, but it wasn't like he could deny the hunger that was eating at him like a worrisome mosquito. Rising off his haunches, he slowly padded back toward the village, trying to prolong the inevitable.

Maybe it was time to head to the city. He and his few friends—more like acquaintances—went to the human settlements a few times a year, tasting the other side of the world. It was fun—the sights, the smells, the foods. And there were plenty of readily available males to cavort with. He'd miss the forests, his home, but the city held wonders for him. *Possibilities.*

Feelings pulled him in ten million different directions as he made his way back to the village.

Chapter Two

Nexhan sighed as he hugged his brothers tightly, their skin smooth and warm against his. So many powerful bodies came up against his, their strength evident as they squeezed him. Laughter rang out and joy permeated the air. Many had dressed for the feast tonight, their bodies runed, their long flowing hair braided and decorated with beads, feathers, leaves. He too had dressed. Nakoda had kept his cabin the same as it had been when he had left. All his belongings were a little dusty but sat quietly in their spots. He had decorated his body with his best paint, the ink made from the berries that grew under *Weynka Le Gai*. He had adorned his locks in beads of obsidian, polished stone and bone, and dressed in his finest pants made from the buttery soft hide of a Totoa, a long-lost creature that resembled a white buffalo.

A squeak cut through the air and a yellow-haired male crashed into him. "*Mi'wisa!*"

Nexhan laughed and embraced his clan brother, running his fingers through his flowing locks. They were warm and bright and reminded him of sunshine on a hot summer day. He took the male's chin in his hand and teased. "Cherchi? I remember you being so much shorter."

"But I have grown! Almost as big as you!" Cherchi growled and slapped Nexhan on the back.

Indeed, he had. Cherchi had been just a cub of fifteen when Nexhan had left all those years ago and he was as bright and cheerful as he had been back then, that smile lighting up the very room. *Glad to know our tragedies haven't dampened his soul...*

Cherchi had grown into a fine young Rune Fang, handsome and stout, and his eyes shone with the life and warmth of the sun, dark rings of yellow outlining their buttery softness.

"You might be bigger, but I'm faster!" He grinned playfully.

Nexhan laughed. That he didn't doubt. Cherchi was as fast as the wind, as swift as the sunrise and could outrun even the quickest bird. Others came to greet Nexhan and to rub their bodies against him in affection. Broan and his son, Nashuk, hugged him tightly. It was almost as though he hadn't left, as though he hadn't been apart from his family for nearly a hundred years. But, it was more than just his clan welcoming him home — it was the Mother, for she was in everything and everyone.

He heard Nakoda tell everyone to settle down, to give Nexhan room to breathe, then he came up next to Nexhan, bumping his shoulder. He leaned in and whispered, "Told you so."

Nexhan simply smiled as the males went about preparing the feast, the gigantic table in the center of the main lodge filling with food. Venison was the main meat, an entire carcass lay upon the center along with whole trout and duck. A feast such as this always represented the four elements. Deer for earth, fish for water, waterfowl for air—and a very potent, yet delicious plate of *pour'rika*, a type of pepper that had the ability to kill a human, represented the element for fire. It was one of the very few traditions that had been brought from their homeland that still existed today. The mingling of scents wafted around Nexhan and he inhaled. He could not remember a feast like this in a long time. Clearly, Hihano had been busy in the kitchen.

Cherchi stood on a chair, hanging a bough of wild lily from a huge chandelier composed entirely of antlers and situated over the table. Males disappeared into the kitchen then emerged with plates of steaming food and desserts piled high. They smiled and laughed at each another, the very essence of life in their eyes.

His brothers. His warriors. He felt pride swell in his heart as he watched his family move about. With his keen eyes, he caught the form of a big male huddled in a dark corner, the shifter's silver hair draped over his face so that his expression couldn't be read. Storm. Nexhan nodded to him, and he nodded back in greeting but looked away quickly. Painful memories assaulted Nexhan. He pushed them away, determined not to let them ruin the night.

The clan link was returning quickly and although it felt lovely, he had almost forgotten that his emotions would be bared to his brothers unless he controlled the link. Seeing this, Storm retreated. Nexhan wanted to reach out, to hold the male close to him, to breath in his wild scent, but he knew it wouldn't help. In reality, a hundred years had passed, but for them it made no difference. Time could not heal their wounds.

Sensing Nexhan's desires, Nakoda leaned in. "He doesn't come around very often. We miss him."

"He hasn't forgiven himself," Nexhan stated. He wasn't sure if he was speaking of Storm or himself.

"No. Often, that is the hardest thing to do," Nakoda, ever the wise, whispered.

Nexhan made a silent promise to speak with Storm later. He needed to put into words his feelings toward the man. Nexhan had never blamed the male, but he wouldn't deny that seeing the Rune Fang's face brought to light the painful memories of the past. Storm's twin brother, Rain, had betrayed the clan out of jealousy, ushering in one of the worst massacres in their long history, effectively thinning their numbers by half and taking their remaining six females — including Nexhan's mother and his intended breed-mate.

Nexhan sighed and scanned the faces of his brothers, but there was one face he did not see. He asked Nakoda, "Where is Shenwok? I haven't sensed his presence yet."

Nakoda stiffened and a shadow passed over his face. Shifters were blessed with good hearing and everyone turned to regard Nakoda, their faces falling, their heads bowing. Nakoda cleared his throat and placed a calloused palm against Nexhan's back. "Our brother left us. Several years ago."

Nexhan's breath punched out of his lungs as he searched his friend's face. "How?"

"Kaga. He died protecting the clan," Nakoda stated. Kaga were their mortal — or immortal, as it were — enemies. They were demons, terrible and powerful that could usurp the power of a shifter much like a vampire to a human. It was not a pleasant death.

Sensing Nexhan's next question, Nakoda said, "It was a quick death, for he passed from mortal wounds and not the theft of his magic. He was not alone."

Which was a huge relief. To have one's magic raped from him was considered a fate worse than death itself. Nexhan looked into Nakoda's beautiful eyes as they shimmered with moisture, and he understood. It was okay to miss a loved one—to want to hold the dear one once again, if only for a few minutes, but it wasn't healthy to mourn the person for there was no true death, only change. Shenwok had simply gone with the Mother and that was a good thing.

Nexhan nodded and smiled. "Then we shall feast in his honor tonight as well."

A round of shouts went up in agreement before his brothers resumed their chores.

The door to the lodge creaked open and a male, Mewah, his flowing hair like the autumn sky colored with leaves, rushed to a woman carrying a child. She smiled shyly at him and Mewah supported her as he urged her toward Nexhan. Nexhan instinctively caught her energy waves and read them as a cat reads the scents in the winds. She wasn't quite shifter, but she was runed lightly. And she was beautiful. Long, flowing auburn hair curled around her shoulders and she had a perfect oval face highlighted by two chocolate brown eyes that would melt any male's heart.

"*Mi'wisa,* this is my mate, Caroline." He smiled brightly, his teeth showing, his face full of love. "And my son, Adam. He is eight cycles of the moon."

Nexhan looked at her, surprised, then he understood. She had no magic about her, not the kind that flowed through shifters. "You are human."

She nodded. "Believe me, it is a shock to me that this is all real—that you are all real. I'm certain it's the same for you, considering what my Mew has told me."

Nexhan snapped his mouth shut and mentally bonked himself in the head." Forgive me. That was rude." He took her hand and kneeled, whispering ancient words of praise and pledges against her soft skin.

"Oh, I don't think I'll ever get use to this." She grinned at her mate then winked. "However, I can't complain about all the eye candy."

Everyone laughed and many blushed. To shifters, nudity wasn't frowned upon, and they had a habit of parading around in little or nothing at all, but to be praised, especially about your assets by a female, was a great thing indeed.

Nexhan rose to his feet, feeling as astonished as everyone else. The birth of a Rune Fang was a rare and cherished event and even more amazing given that the mother was human. There was some human blood in the clan, but not much. This union of Mewah and Caroline was nothing short of a miracle.

"Ah, shouldn't we be the ones bowing to you?" she asked uncertainly, looking at her mate.

"Sorry, I should have explained our customs to you better. I was just so excited with our *Mi'wisa's* return then you tackled me..." Mewah's cheeks reddened as he realized what he was saying and everyone chuckled.

Nexhan smiled at Caroline. "I think what Mewah means to say is that people do not serve a leader. Their leader serves his people. May I?"

She nodded and he gently laid a kiss on her forehead. "My sister."

36

The baby picked that time to burble something. He looked at the child snuggled against her shoulder. "He is a gift from the Mother."

"Would you like to hold him?" she asked, moving the babe into his arms.

Nexhan couldn't help the grin on his face. Many of the males had come to join him and watched eagerly as if they, too, wanted a turn as he picked up the little boy. Cubs weren't raised only by their parents but by the entire clan. He held him high in the air. At first, the baby squeaked in protest from being separated from his mother then he smiled down at Nexhan with the eyes of his father.

"Not only do we feast of Shenwok but also this gift of life." He growled and the child laughed, reaching a pudgy hand out to bop Nexhan on the forehead.

Everyone laughed. But, babes were as fickle as the wild storms and Adam began to fuss, his face twisting into unhappiness. Nexhan placed a kiss on the boy's forehead then handed him back to Caroline, who cuddled him close to her breast.

"Has a welcoming ceremony been performed yet?" Nexhan asked.

Mewah cleared his throat and looked at Nakoda before answering. "Ah, no…"

"Then upon the next full moon, we shall present the babe to the Mother and welcome him into our family. Tomorrow, send word to the neighboring clans. All are invited to witness this miracle," Nexhan declared and his brothers shouted in agreement. Nexhan looked at Caroline. "Will you be wintering with us?"

It was Mewah who answered. "Yes. We've decided to stay here until Adam is old enough to travel then we have made plans to lodge in the village during the warm months and hole up in the city during the cooler months." He looked at his mate tenderly, who was desperately trying to get Adam to settle down. "I could not ask her to abandon her family for mine."

Nexhan nodded.

Caroline tried to say something over the wailing of her babe but Adam had lungs that would rival any raptor-shifter. That was good. It was a sign of health. Several males surrounded her and cooed at the baby, making faces, trying to get him to settle while the others finished preparing the feast.

"What is wrong, little one?" Mewah asked his son.

A new scent caught Nexhan's attention—no, not new—just a scent he hadn't become familiar with yet. It was clean and spicy like mint almost, a sweet crispness...

The cougar-shifter walked in and Caroline squeaked.

"My favorite kitty!" She smiled warmly then plopped Adam into the male's arms. A pet name like that would probably offend most men, but the shifter simply smiled brightly.

The babe instantly quieted as he pawed at Cole's face.

Nexhan had expected a boy, but what he got was a handsome young man, taller than most cougar-shifters and leanly muscular. He had the sandy hair that was common amongst his species but it was cut short, unlike the Rune Fang who often grew their hair to ankle length. Cole had retained those same violet eyes that seemed as deep as the sky itself. He wore modern-day clothing—a gray T-shirt with the word 'Affliction' printed across it and black jeans. He even had a piercing in his left lobe, which was a peculiarity among shifters. He carefully avoided eye contact with

Nexhan as he smiled softly at the babe, who had begun to burble happily in his arms.

Caroline made a noise of supreme pleasure. "You are a miracle! I don't understand how you do it."

Adam agreed and beamed with his pudgy little cheeks, bonking Cole in the nose with one hand.

The cougar grinned slyly. "I'm just cute."

Chuckling, Nokoda said, "Cole, this is our brother, Nexhan. Come, officially greet him."

Cole gave Nokoda a no-shit look then blushed slightly as he regarded Nexhan. "Hey."

Nexhan nodded, not sure what to say. He watched the cougar-shifter intently as he coddled the babe. There was suddenly a mask of arrogance around Cole as if he didn't care who Nexhan was, but when he caught Nexhan watching him, he flushed and turned the other way, making cooing noises at Adam, who ate up the attention.

Sensing that Nokoda wanted to say something about Cole's subtle disrespect, Nexhan decided to remain silent, the mood too good to ruin with trivial things.

Someone patted him hard on the back. It was Hihano, his bright orange eyes aglow. "Shall we eat?"

There was a collective, joyful shout.

* * * *

The feast had gone well. There had been laughter, conversation, songs sung. Caroline and Mewah recounted how they had met. She had been a mycologist working in Redwood National Park at the time and Mewah had been so taken by her, he had trailed her for days, finally finding the courage to initiate contact. It was an interesting story, made more appealing by the way they kept finishing each other's sentences and smiling at each other—true mates. Adam had been passed around, the males trying to get him to lose his fussiness. To no one's surprise, he ended up in Cole's lap and had eventually fallen fast asleep. Caroline had taken her leave at that time, along with the babe, kissing Cole on the head as she'd left. Mewah followed shortly after.

Storm had made a single appearance during the evening, a plate in his hand as he loaded it with food. Then with a polite greeting to Nexhan, he'd disappeared for the rest of the night. Nexhan had hoped to see him again, wanted to start some sort of conversation, but Storm seemed disinterested.

Soon it had come time for drink and stories, and Nexhan was the main attraction.

What was the city like?

What were the humans like?

Where did you go?

Did you climb the metal trees?

It went on and on, Nexhan recounting his tales until his mouth ran dry, his brothers watching him with big eyes. He told them about the wonders of humanity, their technology but what really seemed to interest his brothers was his time spent with the Loupen. The Loupen were once Fenrir, great wolf-shifters and the royal hunters of the Mother Goddess. They had been twisted by demons into what was commonly referred to as werewolves by mankind. They had been on this earth for thousands of years, almost as long as the shifters, but they tended to keep to themselves. Most shifters viewed them as monstrosities, a corruption of nature and bane to the natural order. Nexhan had carried the belief as well, at least until he'd spent some time with them.

Nexhan smiled. "They are not as our stories have made them to be. They afforded me respect and kindness as well as companionship. Initially, I sensed the inherent darkness within, but they have proven many times over to be honorable and fair."

More questions followed about the Loupen, but Nexhan left the topic, focusing on the rogue shifters he had met on his journeys. It seemed, though, the more he spoke, the more he piqued his brothers' curiosity. He felt the unspoken questions hovering in the air.

Did you find them?

Did you kill them?

He was glad no one found the courage to voice their questions.

Nexhan had his own questions, though. *Is the reward of vengeance worth the price of family?*

He had shared some of his belongings with them, his cell phone being the main curiosity amongst the younger males. It was a newer model and had come equipped with games the humans called apps. Cherchi had hogged it the entire time, growling with enthusiasm every time he gained a level. Nexhan was surprised that they got reception out here, but Nakoda had explained that he had climbed *Weynka Le Gai* to erect an antenna. Everyone laughed softly as the male blushed and commented absently that he would have made a horrible raptor-shifter.

Eventually the feast ended and it had come time to run. He bade his brothers to meet him in the forest, for he had something to do. He made his way over to the First Daughter quickly, eager to put his sorrow behind him and join his brothers under the night sky, racing the very wind.

The giant sequoia loomed above him, its body stretching to the sky, giving the impression that one could climb to the clouds upon its branches. He pressed his palm against the rough bark and admired the grooves. When his fingers found the first of the names carved into the tree, he sighed. He passed the dozens of names, males and females, sons, daughters, fathers and mothers and…lovers. All were etched permanently into *Weynka Le Gai*. Sometimes when he was a cub, Nexhan swore he could hear their whispering voices on the gentle breeze, as if they floated above, watching over their loved ones.

Nexhan found Shenwok's name, the last one etched into the tree. He fingered it gently, whispering prayers, hoping the male would hear him. "I'm sorry I wasn't here for you. I should have been. But there were things I thought I needed to do, things I thought would help heal my wounds. I think I was wrong, though, all those years desperate for vengeance when I should have been here. I was selfish. I wasn't the only one who had lost so much. I hope, when we meet again in the Mother's garden, you can forgive me."

Voicing the truths he'd never had the courage to say before cleansed him in a way he hadn't thought possible. It was as though all the anger had poured out of him like hot tears, leaving a gentle calm inside him. He circled the tree, his fingers grazing the names of dozens of the Rune Fangs he'd known. He passed his breed-mate, lingered there for a second, caressing the elegant script, then found the names of his parents. He made a silent vow to correct his past mistakes and give them a reason to be proud of him.

Nexhan swallowed a lump as he fell to his knees and pressed his lips to a name that seemed as old as time. The person it had belonged to now felt like a dream to him, a fantasy, a memory that drifted along the endless expanse of time until Nexhan wasn't sure if the person had ever been real or not. He whispered dear words, words of affection and promises, and it was almost as if he were kissing more than a name. But, that was the way of *Weynka Le Gai*. When one died, they were buried at the tree's roots to become one with the Mother, forever held in her delicate embrace. Part of what the name had once been was now in the bark where Nexhan pressed lips.

He was unable to stop the stream of tears gliding down his cheeks. When he had left, he'd put his emotions away and honed his mind, heart and body for vengeance. Now that his enemies were dead and he was home again, the memories and emotions of the past hurtled toward him, a tornado whipping up all the pain he had buried in his mind.

The distant sound of free flowing water…

The scent of wild flowers and his lover in his nose…

A gorgeous smile…

"Hey there, big boy…"

A twig snapped under a heavy weight. Nexhan jerked his head up.

Cole stopped in his tracks and swallowed hard. "Oh, sorry. I didn't know anyone was here."

Nexhan stood and let the male see his emotions. It wasn't like he could hide them anyway, and maybe he didn't want to. Cole stood there for a moment, looking around, uncertain. Nexhan hoped the cougar might offer him some sort of comfort. After so long in the human world, he was desperate for the touch of another shifter. He wanted to feel a warm body embracing him, letting him cry out his hurt. But Cole was of a different clan, so clearly such actions would have been inappropriate—wouldn't they? Though the different species tended to separate themselves from one another, the various clans had always been friendly and affection was openly given and accepted.

Stop thinking like a human. "It's okay," Nexhan said softly, unsure if he was trying to console himself or the other male. "I was just saying good-bye to my brother."

"Was he your brood-brother?" Cole asked softly.

"No. Still, the hurt goes deep," He patted his chest. When the cougar didn't say anything, Nexhan asked, "Will you be joining in our run?"

A patch of red crept up into the male's cheeks. He sputtered, "Uh... I..."

"You are welcome to."

Cole took a step back and tangled a foot in a root, falling on his ass. He looked wide-eyed at Nexhan then stumbled to his feet again, trying to retreat.

Nexhan called out for him, but Cole was quick and disappeared into the night.

He sighed wearily and cast one last, longing look at the names carved into *Weynka Le Gai*. Resigned, he padded off toward the forest to join his brothers. He needed their strength and their love.

Chapter Three

Cole sighed as he listened to the shuffling and padding of a dozen or so sets of paws. He was perched in between two large roots, just staring off in the direction of where the clan was. The Rune Fang were on the move, their joyous growls and moans echoing through the forest like a chorus of wolves singing praise to the moon god. The waves of energy assaulted him with overwhelming feelings of love and happiness. It nearly made him sick. How the hell could they be so carefree while their species teetered on the brink of extinction?

Cole tsked at himself for being so negative. They had a right to be happy, he supposed. Their clan leader had returned. But the mushy feelings were roiling through him and he couldn't help but begrudge them their happiness—because he wanted it, envied it. He wondered what it would feel like to be accepted so fully, to be welcomed home like that with bear hugs and shouts of glee. It was such a strange concept to him that he couldn't even imagine it. He wanted to be a worthy, contributing member so badly he could taste it.

He sighed again and picked at stray grass blades intending to eat them, but finding that he didn't have much of an appetite. He'd eaten very little at the feast, just pushed around scraps of meat and other things that on any other day he would have devoured.

Why am I such a loser? Did I do something awful in my previous life?

He sat downwind, so he didn't catch the scent, but he felt the presence behind him. He turned to regard Storm—the male leaning against a tree, his thick arms folded over his broad chest, watching Cole intently with those silver eyes that glowed like lightning. His hair blew lightly in the breeze loose around his face, the locks a perfect resemblance of the wild thunderclouds, all light, dark gray and shadowy blue intermingling to frame a handsome yet harsh face. Cole had no idea what was up with the guy. He was creepy and elusive, only making an appearance every now and then to help with his share of the chores.

Cole ignored him and leaned back against the tree. He felt as if he were being cradled like a child, the soft moss covering the rough bark like cool, comfortable sheets.

He had never really understood the deep connection the Rune Fang had with the Mother Goddess. Maybe it was because most modern-day shifters had slowly begun to drift away from nature and toward the world of man and technology. Perhaps it was the smidgen of human blood in him, but being here like this… It was almost if she were holding him. Goddess, he wished he could feel his mother's smaller frame against his own again. He missed his parents—he really did—but he couldn't watch the shadow of disappointment cross his father's face anymore. It hurt too much.

Cole munched on the blade of grass, the flavor tangy and slightly sweet. Shifters had different palates than humans and to him it tasted fantastic, like rich earth — if life could even be tasted.

A growl caught his attention followed by a wave of playful energy. He must have sighed or done something to make his longing obvious, because he felt the disapproval of Storm behind him.

Cole understood what the male was getting at and snapped back, "Don't start! I don't see you out there with them!"

Strangely, Cole had never uttered a word to Storm before, nor had the man attempted any sort of contact with him either. Cole had only run into him a few times and at each encounter, Storm had just glared as though he didn't want Cole there. So now his first words were spoken in anger. He hadn't meant to come off so pissy, but he wanted to be alone and not be bothered with the obvious.

Storm's silver eyes flared in the moonlight like a slow curling bolt of lightning streaking across the sky. It told Cole that the male didn't care to have the obvious pointed out to him.

Storm's face went blank and he nodded, conceding Cole's point then he turned around and walked off into the woods in the opposite direction of the clan, his tight leather pants hugging his fine ass. Cole adverted his gaze. He wondered if Storm knew about his orientation. If there was one thing he knew about the male, it was that he was perceptive, and the few times Storm had looked at Cole, it seemed as if the male was gazing into his soul. Well, it wouldn't matter either way, but Cole preferred to keep it to himself if possible. But they did have something in common, didn't they?

We're both outsiders.

Cole shrugged and absorbed the ecstatic energy of the clan...and Nexhan's loud roar. Both acceptance and dominance filled it, as if he were simultaneously declaring his position and gathering his people to him in a great big hug. *Nexhan*. Damn, he needed to erase that name from his vocabulary and scrub the image of all that power and beauty from his mind. No good could come from him fantasizing...but, damn, the male was a serious piece of meat. Yeah, that sounded crude, but it was the truth. He'd love to be taken by such...perfection.

Pfft. Like there was any possibility of that, anyway. Sure, shifters had sex with each another for companionship and pleasure, but Cole felt...unworthy. He didn't deserve the attention of a shifter like Nexhan. Look what he had gone a done earlier by making a fool of himself stumbling over his own feet. But, that didn't mean he couldn't dream...

Frustrated and pissed at himself and the unfairness of the world, he got up and made his way through the forest—in the opposite direction of the clan—and Storm. He wanted to be alone with nothing but the reaching trees and the green shrubs to stand witness to his failure. Sometimes he really felt at peace among the silence of the shrubs and trees. He knew it was pointless to feel sorry for himself, but he just didn't care anymore. What else could he possibly do? He knew at this moment that going back to his parents' clan wasn't an option. Never mind that he couldn't marry Bessa or contribute to the clan, but he didn't want to pretend he was something he was not—hetero husband, potential clan leader, parents' pride. He was none of those things and never would be.

Time to move on. He blinked up at the trees disappearing into inky blackness overhead. The sequoias were so tall and thick that he could see neither the stars nor the moon, but he instinctively felt their presence. He remembered the creation story his mother had told him when he was a cub, the same campfire fable that had been told for thousands of years — how the shifters came into being. It was all silliness to him, just a good bedtime story, but he couldn't stop thinking about it. Maybe he just missed the sound of his mother's voice.

According to legend, the shifter race had come into being when the Mother Goddess and the Gray Man mated. There had been only a few shifters at first, but as time went on and the Mother Goddess saw how good her creations were, she mated again with the Gray Man and *voila!* Tigers, cougars, wolves, raptors, even dragons, horses — and so many subspecies a person would need a computer to keep track of them — were born.

Dragons, huh? Sounds like a bunch of bullshit. Though his people were magical in nature, they still had a tendency to whip up imaginary fables.

Why was he thinking about this now? He kicked a loose rock in agitation.

A cawing caught his attention. He looked up and found the source. A huge crow stared down at him from a short branch, its large, inky black eyes blinking at him with curiosity. It cocked its bird head slightly as if it were trying to solve a mystery its inferior brain had no hope of deciphering, but its eyes shone with intelligence. It was larger than a normal crow with fluffy crown feathers that gave it a regal appearance.

Cole's memories swirled, his mother's voice echoing around his brain. The stories she'd told him slowly dripped back into his think tank. *Oketa*. Yeah, that was it. *Oketa* was the name given to the crow—more specifically, a crow in service of the Gray Man. The Native Americans viewed the crow as an omen of things to come. So did shifters, but for an entirely different reason. Most often the *Oketa* was a positive sign, but it all depended on the situation. The faucet in his head must have been set on low, because it was all that he could remember.

"What?" he asked the bird.

It cocked its head to the other side, its shiny feathers glistened in the low light, making it appear as if it were constructed of liquid darkness. Its intelligent eyes watched him carefully, blinking quickly again. It opened its dagger-like beak and cawed once then flew a short distance to a neighboring branch. It watched him expectantly.

Cole sighed. It wasn't unusual for an animal to act this way around a shifter. The wild beasts sensed the magic inside them and were sometimes drawn to it.

The crow ruffled its feathers then cawed again. Cole ignored it and continued on his way, not really sure where he was headed. He could still hear the clan shuffling around, could still feel the refreshing waves of their energy, and he wanted desperately to join them. The bird tailed him, hopping to one branch after another, blinking at him with those oil-drop eyes.

Cole spun around when it cawed at him and shouted, "*What?*"

The beastie simply turned its head. Cole let out a big breath. Maybe the bird was hungry or something? Occasionally, a starving animal entered the village in search of food and the Rune Fangs fed them. Perhaps the bird was a regular customer and recognized Cole's animalistic energies.

"Sorry, I don't have anything for you," Cole said softly.

The crow simply shifted its head to the other side.

He rolled his eyes and shook his head. Where exactly was he going? Well, it didn't matter. He slid his T-shirt over his head and pulled down his jeans. He wasn't wearing any underwear—most shifters didn't. He folded his clothes neatly and placed them in a bag that had been stuck in his pocket, along with a bracelet made of leather and metal spikes that an acquaintance had bought for him on their last trip to the city. He tucked everything under a root. The most skilled of shifters could retain a holding of their human bodies along with whatever possessions might be on it, but Cole, like everything else, lacked that talent.

He felt the moon's presence climbing higher in the sky. Its light had just begun to puncture the thick canopy and filter down through the trees in soft silvery ribbons. He didn't need much light, though. He cracked his neck side to side, rolled his shoulders and let the change come upon him. He needed a distraction from his miseries, but most of all he needed to prove to himself that he was still shifter and not just a magicless, clumsy mess.

He shivered, but it wasn't from any chill. His skin grew light and sensitive and his insides felt like they were floating. He went blind, but only for a millisecond. When his sight returned, everything seemed much taller. But it was his perception that had shifted. He shook his reformed body in an effort to rid himself of the lingering aftereffects that were nothing more than an annoying tingle.

The crow cawed at him.

Cole looked at the bird through cat eyes then hissed at it in an attempt to get it to go away. The thing simply squawked back. Frustrated with his shadow, he roared at it, a high growl that carried through the trees. The bird cawed loudly and flapped its wings but stayed perched on its branch.

In defeat, Cole plopped his hind quarters on the turf. He sat there for a while, mulling over the emotions roiling through him. He was of a mind to keep walking through the night and through the day, straight into the city of Los Angeles. At the very least, he'd be able to get laid there—no questions, no worries. Among the humans, he was a god. Every gay man and hetero woman wanted him. It was why he liked the cities so much. Here, with his own kind, he was weak and a disappointment. What would anyone in their right mind chose?

Cole got up on his paws and started padding southward. The bird loomed overhead, watching him with smart eyes, hopping branches whenever Cole got far enough away, and offering a caw or two to let him know it was still there.

He wasn't sure how far he'd walked, but the moon slowly dipped to the west and its yellow-gold light turned to that of twilight. Soon, the sun peeked over the eastern horizon, though he couldn't see it through the thick trees. He walked until he could no longer feel the clan. Had Nexhan come this way when he had left all those years ago? Had he looked back with sadness as he'd left his family? Or had he run for the city with determination set in his heart, never looking back? Why did he even leave in the first place? Cole had asked Nakoda that once, but the male never answered.

Cole wanted to know. He didn't know why he did. He just...*wanted* to know. Maybe he was searching for some sort of kinship with the man. *Bleh – yeah, right.* He was more likely to find a smidgen of camaraderie with Storm than the leader of the Rune Fangs.

The bird cawed at him then took to the air, beating its wings furiously as it set off into the trees.

Yeah, good riddance, featherbrain. That incessant croak had started to get on his nerves, but for some reason he found himself drifting toward the bird. He came to a large clearing surrounded by tall trees and stood there, looking around, sniffing the air. The crow was nowhere in sight.

Something stung him in the hindquarters and he jerked. Some sort of neon orange, feathery thingamabob was sticking out of his ass!

What the fu –

He didn't have time to finish that thought. It was almost instantaneous. A thick, deep drowsiness hit him and he hissed at the empty air. His ears detected voices nearby, frantic, excited but careful. Humans. He'd been darted! He raised his head to the air and let out a long, screeching roar.

He cursed the crow. He cursed himself. He cursed the entire fucking world as things went dark.

Stupid bird. So much for good omens.

* * * *

Nexhan buried his face against the warm body wrapped around him. The soft fur against the naked skin of his nose and the scent that filled him seemed faintly floral, as if the wind carried the fragrance of dozens of different flowers to him. Cherchi. Nexhan put a paw around the smaller body and the young male purred in response. Cherchi was slight of frame for a Rune Fang, but that was because he was young and, as he aged, his cat would fill out more. Nexhan felt the weight and heat of a larger cat against his back and instantly recognized Nakoda's scent—a mix of pungent, yet pleasant, herbs.

They had run long and hard all night under the watchful gaze of the sequoias. They'd play-fought and roamed the woods for miles, crossing the river and roaring in celebration. Only when the sky grew light did they fall against one another in exhaustion. It had been… There were no words to describe the feelings coursing through him. The sensation was akin to the sun rising over the wide, wild ocean on a warm summer's day, painting the sky and clouds as if they were a great canvas. It was like the early days of spring, where the first warm breeze chased away the chill, the flowers bloomed brightly and the birds sang sweet songs. And, it was like being with the ones he loved on a cold winter's night, sharing each other's body heat and reveling in each other's presence. But no, that was not enough to describe what he was feeling now. There was one regret, though, and it was a painful shard in his chest cavity. Storm had been absent. Storm should have been with them, sharing in their delight, their love, but he had retreated deep into the forest. Nexhan had kept an eye out for the cougar too, hoping Cole would have joined them in their run. He would have been welcomed openly but he too had disappeared.

Nakoda shifted behind him and licked Nexhan's ear with a sandpaper tongue that pulled at the fur. Nexhan opened his eyes, squinting at the brightness. His brothers lazed around the clearing, their bodies entangled with one another. Nexhan unsheathed his claws and lightly sank them into Cherchi's sandy coat, the thick fur absorbing the sharp points. The male stirred and rolled over onto his back, exposing his belly, paws in the air. He chuffed a playful good morning.

Nexhan got to his feet and shook the debris from his body.

Soft laughter wafted around him as the rest of the clan began to come to, their faces reflections of sheer happiness. Some even appeared drunk, smiling dumbly and looking up into the trees with wistful expressions.

Nakoda joined him and rubbed his head against Nexhan's body, whipping the air with his tail then curling around Nexhan's back. Nexhan could feel the shift clawing at his body, making tiny rips, urging him to let his human side out. He knew his friends were feeling the same thing. Nakoda and Cherchi had been the closest to him, so their energy fed from his and the clan magic that was reawakening had allowed him to stay in his cat form much longer, even through sleep.

A pair of arms came around his neck and one of the older males, Broan, scrubbed his head voraciously in greeting. "Morning, *Mi'wisa*."

Nexhan chuffed and pushed his body playfully against Broan, effectively knocking the male on his ass. Broan laughed, as did several others. Their human bodies might be big, but their cats were bigger, bulkier and could throw weight around with the best of them. He looked at his brothers, most of them on their feet now, and prepared himself for the change. His stomach rumbled, demanding food and he was sure the others were as equally hungry. They had expended a lot of energy during the night, even after putting away all those calories.

Nexhan let the warmth spread through him...

He suddenly stilled, as did the others.

Everyone looked to the treetops, where the light had begun to stream down in a soft hazy blue. The wind picked up slightly, its fingers weaving their selves down through the branches to stroke Nexhan's fur. Along with the breeze came the shuffling of leaves and the soft creak of wood. It slowly built to a steady and soothing hum.

"The trees speak," someone muttered, awestruck.

"There is a message on the wind." Nexhan wouldn't have been shocked to hear Storm's voice if it weren't for the breeze carrying distant words to them. The male came out from behind a young redwood, his form cloaked in black leather pants, his hair loose and slinking around his face like wind-swept clouds. His gaze remained on the ground, as if he couldn't bear to see anyone.

Nexhan was glad to look upon him, but at the moment his mind was on the event. When was the last time the forest had spoken to them? *Not for a long time, not since...*

He abandoned that thought and listened carefully as did everyone else, no one moving except to turn their heads as the wind whirled around them, the sounds of the forest filling the clearing. It was a subtle song of whispered words and to a human it would sound like nothing more than the rustle of leaves. To magic-endowed beings it was much more. The words were eloquent, soft and fluid like a gentle stream, but utterly foreign to Nexhan. He wasn't old enough to know the language spoken before time was time but there were plenty of tales, though. Once when the earth was young and life was innocent and free, the trees had talked openly, laughed and told their own stories. But that seemed more of a bedtime story than anything else. However, the trees were speaking once again... If only he could understand their words.

Cherchi came into Nexhan's view and relayed the message, *"What are they saying?"*

Several heads turned to regard Nexhan but he had no answer. From what he did understand, dread came along with the message. He blew out a big breath then looked at Nakoda then to Cherchi, both still in their cats, their expressions reflecting the same uneasiness roiling through him. They were stronger this way, more agile and better able to defend the village against an attack. The others were in human form now and likely too tired to shift back. He looked over where Storm had been, but the male was gone. Nexhan growled softly to himself, wishing that the wild winds didn't carry the male away so often, but that was the nature of the element of air.

"Mi'wisa?" Broan asked, looking for guidance.

I'm clan leader. It was Nexhan's choice on how they should proceed.

Everyone looked at him in expectation.

He sent his thoughts to his brothers, *"I do not understand the trees' words, but I feel deep in my heart that they speak of something ill. Where is Mewah?"*

"With Caroline and the little one," Broan replied. "He returned to the village to be with them when everyone was settling down for the night."

"Good. Nakoda, Cherchi and I shall scout the forest surrounding the village. I want everyone to return to Weywoni Le Gai *and be diligent until we return. And no one is to wander around alone. If something needs to be done, move in pairs. Protect Mewah's mate and the cub."*

"Do you think it is Kaga?" Cherchi asked, looking startled, the mixture of sandy fur and sienna stripes seeming to pale with his worry.

"The trees did not warn us last time," Nashuk, Broan's son, said. "Why would they do so now?"

"I don't feel the presence of Kaga, but let us be safe," Nexhan said.

Everyone began moving toward the village. A few had asked to join in on the scouting mission, but Nexhan ordered that they return to protect Mewah's mate and child. Besides, the more bodies with him, the more a chance of detection if it were indeed Kaga. They had accepted his explanation and in return, he'd promised he would send for help if the situation was too dire. The instinct of the clan was to protect their clan leader, especially strong, capable warriors such as the ones surrounding him now, but Nexhan felt that it was his duty to protect *them.* He knew his logic was sound. Caroline and Adam were their priority.

Nexhan watched until the last male disappeared around the trunk of a redwood.

Nakoda walked around to look him in the eye, his broad form eating up much of Nexhan's view. *"We are with you,* Mi'wisa."

Nexhan let himself drown in his friend's warm, golden eyes. He had almost forgotten what it felt like to be connected, to know that there were people who had your back no matter what, who were willing to give their lives for you. And he would give his life for them, no questions asked. He nodded then looked at Cherchi, who returned his glance with eagerness at having been chosen to assist in their investigation.

"Come," Nexhan urged, *"let us see what we can find."*

They filed through the forest, Nexhan leading with Cherchi behind him and Nakoda at Cherchi's rear, almost as if protecting him. A Rune Fang was still considered young until the one-hundredth year and Cherchi was only a few years over that milestone.

They moved silently as their paws hit the turf, the soft dirt absorbing their weight. Nexhan led them slowly but surely through the younger redwoods around the village, reading the energy prints, searching for the vile and black presence of Kaga. With the other's help, Nexhan kept a close eye out for any signs of Kaga potholes — small patches of blackened and rotting earth where the demons emerged. Nexhan listened to the trees, their words slowly drifting away, carried away by the wind. He wondered if it was the untamed wind that had awoken the forest or if the forest had used the breeze to carry their message.

When there was no upset to the village's border, Nexhan led his brothers deeper into the forest, the trees growing taller and their bodies thicker, wider. He took in the scents of the forest floor, rubbing himself against the trees, not only to spread his scent but also to connect with them. They had grown silent again as surely as though they'd never spoken at all. Still, he marched on in wide circles, getting farther and farther from the village. They walked so long and so far that his paws began to ache. The urge to change had become a bothersome itch and he knew his brothers were experiencing the same thing.

"I do not sense Kaga or any other wicked things and we have come so far from Weywoni Le Gai," Nakoda sent his waves to Nexhan.

Nexhan stopped and looked up at the reaching sequoias, perking his ears in expectancy. The trees said nothing. Unsure of what to do, he turned to Cherchi and Nakoda. Their expressions remained calm, attentive, as they awaited any order he was prepared to give.

"Let us go closer to the river, and if we do not find any signs, then we shall return to the village," he said.

Nexhan turned south for the river, and it wasn't long before he finally caught the scent of something that interested him. He followed the short trail to a younger tree and used his claws to dig out a plastic bag containing human clothing.

"That is Cole's," Nakoda informed him.

"Indeed." It was only then that Nexhan began to worry about the cougar-shifter. If a Kaga was about then a young cougar was no match for the vile thing. Kaga were slight of form, humanoid, but they were immensely powerful and if the creature locked its jaws into Cole, he'd likely never get away. The demon would feed until it had sucked the last of Cole's life-force out of him. It was a horrid death Nexhan wouldn't wish on anyone. He prayed to the Mother Goddess not to let that be the case.

Nexhan rubbed his neck against the tree and sank his claws into the thick bark, seeking any sort of communion. The trees had spoken before, so why were they speechless now?

The cawing of a crow caught his attention and they all looked in unison to the high boughs of the sequoias. The bird flapped its wings, looking down at them from a stubby branch. It blinked its oil-drop eyes at them, watching them closely.

"Oketa?" Cherchi asked.

The bird took off toward the south.

The two Rune Fangs looked at Nexhan. Crows were common but a sighting could mean anything. It could just be that the bird was searching for food and had been attracted to their shifter magic. It could also mean absolutely nothing.

The crow cawed in the distance, as though urging them to follow.

Or it could mean everything.

Cursing to himself, Nexhan headed toward the south, trotting softly, but urgently. His clan brothers followed.

* * * *

Nexhan watched Cole closely as he stirred in the bed. It had only been a short while since they had brought him back with Nakoda and Cherchi flanking Nexhan as he carried the unconscious cougar upon his shoulders. Even though Cole was young, his cougar had been large and heavy but limp. As they'd settled him in bed, Cole slowly began to stir, which was good. The tranquilizer wouldn't be in his system much longer.

Apparently, still believing he was in his cat body, Cole bared his teeth. His face was a mask of anger, frustration and a bit of fear.

"Cole," Nakoda whispered softly, trying not to startle him. "You're back in the village. Wake up."

"Nakoda?" Cole croaked hoarsely.

"Yeah. You're safe," Nakoda replied stiffly.

Everyone was silent as Cole lolled his head and rubbed his eyes. Slowly he sat up then blinked at them as though he thought he was dreaming or trying to figure out if they were really there. He furrowed his brows, his sandy hair sticking up every which way.

Nexhan had to admit to himself, that he looked adorable so disheveled, but he quickly abandoned that thought as silly. Now was not the time to entertain such ideas.

"What happened?" Cole asked, beleaguered.

Nakoda spoke up. "We found you far from the village. You had been darted by a human research team. Luckily for you, their only interest was to collar and tag you for the sake of science."

Cole looked from Nakoda to Nexhan with those big violet marbles of his and his cheeks flushed as he realized what had happened. He promptly hitched the blanket up over his bare chest and looked away. It was a human motion that didn't surprise Nexhan all that much. Nexhan sensed Nakoda's frustration next to him as Nakoda ground his molars. He focused his attention on the radio collar encircling Cole's neck. The scientists had pierced Cole's ear with a big, red tag too. It would have been funny, but everyone was of a mind not to embarrass the cougar-shifter any more than he already was.

Cole fingered the ear tag.

"Didn't I tell you to mind your surroundings, boy?" Nakoda finally barked. "And why were you so far from the village? You're lucky we found you when we did and chased the humans off! What if they had wicked intentions? What if you'd shifted while unconscious? Are you aware of the mess you could have made?"

"Okay!" Cole snarled and plastered an arrogant mask on his face.

Nexhan placed a hand on Nakoda's shoulder and Nakoda closed his mouth, but his body remained tense with anger. He wanted to press the point, his eyes shining with understanding. Cole had learned his lesson and no amount of chiding would drill the point home better than that collar around his neck and the tag in his ear.

Nexhan motioned to Cherchi, who came forward with a pair of wire cutters and handed them over, his face bright with eagerness at having been of use. Cole looked away again, his face the color of a late-summer strawberry. Nexhan leaned in and Cole let him cut the tag from his ear. This close, Nexhan sensed the tension in the young man. He could smell that sweet spiciness of Cole, and Nexhan would be a liar if he said it didn't stir him in the right way. He finally had a name for it — peppermint.

Cole hissed softly then blotted at the wound on his ear, a small smear of blood coating his hand.

"It will heal in no time," Nexhan said, trying to reassure the young male. He then cut through the thick nylon of the collar and handed it to Cherchi. "Take this deep into the woods then leave it out in the open. Make it appear as if it had been chewed off. And take a friend." Nexhan felt confident that the trees' warning had been about the humans and not something more sinister. Why the presence of humans had awoken the trees, he wasn't sure, but they had scouted a good distance from the village without a trace of Kaga.

The young Rune Fang beamed at him and rushed off to do the task.

Nexhan looked back to Cole, who stared solemnly at a hole in the floorboards. Nexhan turned to regard Nakoda, his aggravated expression stalling Nexhan's words. Honestly, he had no idea what to say or do.

"Cole?" Nakoda ground out.

"What." He pouted.

"What happened?" He softened his tone.

The cougar simply shrugged. "I don't know."

"How can you possibly *not* know?" Nakoda growled.

"Just leave me alone! What do you care anyway?" Cole snarled back, folding his arms across his chest in a defiant pose.

Nakoda sighed disgustedly then squeezed Nexhan's shoulder, taking his leave. Nexhan looked at Storm, who huddled in a dark corner. The male had met them halfway after Nexhan had sent Cherchi back to the village with the news they'd discovered Cole lying limp, surrounded by human researchers.

Storm had assured Nexhan that the trees did not speak of Kaga. In fact, he had mused, it wasn't the trees talking at all. Nexhan wasn't sure what that meant, but he trusted the male's word.

The look Nexhan gave Storm was intense. Somehow, Storm got the idea and made for the door. Nexhan reached out to him, but Storm evaded contact and Nexhan couldn't deny the spear of hurt that it thrust into his chest. Didn't Storm know that he didn't blame him for what had happened all those years ago?

"I need to speak with you," Nexhan said tightly then glanced at Cole. "But later."

"*Mi'wisa.*" Storm nodded then beat feet out of the cabin.

Geez, the way Storm had been avoiding Nexhan since his return, someone might think he smelled bad or something. Nexhan sighed with all the weight of the world on his shoulders as he watched Cole pretend he wasn't there. He had no idea what to say to the cougar. He wanted to ease Cole somehow but knew any mention of the accident would just make Cole feel worse and honestly, Nexhan wasn't in the mood to be snapped at. He didn't trust himself not to throttle the cougar for his impudence.

Frustrated with himself and his own attraction, he shook his head and left.

Chapter Four

Cole had been fighting back the tears that had been pricking the back of his eyes all afternoon. He felt so embarrassed, so...useless. How could he have let humans trap him like that? *Stupid bird.* He knew deep down that he didn't have anyone to blame except himself. He had forgotten to reapply the wards and he hadn't been paying attention to his surroundings, too lost in his own thoughts. What was worse than being collared and tagged like a common animal though, was having Nexhan see him like that.

Nexhan had lugged his dead weight back. Damn, Cole wished he could remember that, wished he could recall what all that power felt like up against him.

He wanted to beat something up. He wanted to ram his fists into the hard bark of a tree until they bled, because physical pain was easier to deal with than the ache rolling like a truck through his insides. He turned up the volume on his iPod, Phuture Sound's *Come to Me* helping him forget his troubles. Thank God the clan had invested in solar panels or else he wouldn't have been able to charge the battery. If there was one thing he missed from the human cities, it was the music…and the men.

He curled his arms around his knees as he watched the treetops sway gently in the breeze. The day was winding down, the sun dipping behind the redwoods to the west. Soon the ball of light would touch the sea before disappearing completely. Goddess, he *needed* to disappear. He realized at that moment that he would have kept walking if he had not been darted. If things had gone differently, then he'd probably be in a human city right now. Would he have come back? Or, would he have just gone deeper and never looked behind him? There were plenty of shifters who lived in the cities like humans.

Nexhan had mentioned staying with the Loupen for a time. A lot of the shifter clans viewed the werewolves as abominations, but if the Loupen would welcome a Rune Fang into their pack, maybe they'd accept someone like him, too.

More like wishful thinking, buddy.

Cole bumped his head against the cabin wall and closed his eyes, letting the music grab him, the combination of the hard beat and smooth melody calming him. The evening meal would probably be over with by now, and as hungry as he was, he wasn't in the mood to see anyone. Goddess, he didn't know how he was ever going to look at anyone ever again.

Cole sensed the presence of something large and heavy hovering above him. He shut his eyes tighter as the dark scent of wildness filled him. Maybe if he ignored it, it would go away. No such luck. A tug on one of his earbuds forced him to look up into Nexhan's shadowy face, his hair loose around his shoulders, the waves of sapphire cascading down his body. Cole desired to drown himself in them.

Uncomfortable, but not wanting to show just how much the male unsettled him, Cole used his best defense—arrogance. He smirked up at the man. "That's rude."

The Rune Fang regarded him thoughtfully for a moment then said, "So is snapping at someone who is trying to help. Besides, how are you to hear what I have to say with the music so loud?"

Cole huffed and pocketed his iPod. "Maybe I don't want to hear what you have to say."

Nexhan's jaw ticked. Cole knew he was being rude and disrespectful. The male could rip him apart if he really wanted to.

Nexhan arched an eyebrow as if he couldn't believe the way Cole was speaking to him, but Cole was positive there was a hint of amusement on that perfect face. *Well, tough shit.* Nexhan wasn't his clan leader and he wanted to be left alone. But when Cole peered up at him, he realized the man was dressed... A hunt?

He had a long bow slung over his back and a quiver filled with arrows. There was a knapsack of sorts around his shoulder, stuffed with things.

"I want you to come with me." It was a demand, a tone ripe with authority.

"Why? For what?" Cole asked, agitated, and he let Nexhan know it. If he had been in his cat form, he would have spat at him.

"Because I said so," Nexhan growled.

The guy obviously wasn't used to being questioned.

"I don't—"

"Shit happens and I get it, but excuses won't feed the chickens and turn over the hay," Nexhan said simply.

"Shit!" Cole had completely forgotten about his chores. Of course, how could he have done what he was supposed to while unconscious? He got up and made a move toward the stables, but Nexhan put himself in Cole's path.

"It's been taken care of."

"I completely forgot. I seriously didn't mean to," Cole insisted.

"I know. Nakoda attended your duties while you were recovering, so don't you think it would be appropriate to repay his kindness?" Nexhan asked.

Cole considered that for a moment. "What do you want me to do?"

"Follow," he instructed.

Reluctantly, Cole obeyed.

They walked across the grassy field and into the woods, bypassing the saplings. Nexhan remained quiet as he led Cole.

Cole couldn't help asking, "Where are we going?"

Nexhan didn't respond. It was just as well, because Cole was having too good of a time watching the man's ass as they navigated the woods. He had a nice back too, the muscles honed to perfection, each moving like water under his sun-kissed skin. Cole licked his lips, wanting to taste all that inviting flesh.

Caught up in his thoughts, Cole walked right into Nexhan, not realizing that the man had stopped. He could've sworn he'd just collided with a mountain. He muttered an apology, not at all sorry for having been able to feel that body up against his for a fraction of a second.

Nexhan set the bow and quiver down then opened his knapsack, pulling out what appeared to be small bladders constructed from cowhide and short, thick tubes with sharpened tips.

"Have you ever milked a sequoia, Cole?" Nexhan asked, as he lay the equipment out across the turf.

"What?" Cole stumbled over himself. Those words were so mundane, but the way the man had said them, it was like... Goddess, Cole didn't even want to think of that. Then again, maybe it was just him and his gutter-bound mind that had made something out of nothing.

"Collected sap?" Nexhan reiterated and looked up at him with eyes like sparkling liquid jewels.

"Uh... No." Cole scratched the back of his neck awkwardly. "I've gathered honey before, though." He left out the part on how that had been a huge disaster.

Nexhan made a sound of acknowledgment then handed him one of the tubes and a stone carved to resemble a hairbrush or something similar. Cole took them and looked at them, beleaguered.

"Watch closely," Nexhan commanded, rising to his feet with a similar set of tools.

Oh, I'm definitely watching closely.

Cole observed as Nexhan placed the peg against the tree bark then used the stone to hammer it in. His shoulders bunched as he worked and Cole smirked, doing a once-over on the Rune Fang. Nexhan didn't stop the hammering until a bead of amber liquid oozed out of the hole. Cole quickly looked away from the man's ass when Nexhan turned to regard him. There was a moment of silence, Nexhan narrowing his eyes for a moment.

"Now, be sure to tie the bladder securely," Nexhan said.

Cole nodded as the male placed one of the cowhide bags under the peg and tied the drawstring to the tubing. He watched, fascinated, as a drop of sap fell into the bag. Images flashed through his mind... He wanted to smear it all over the male and lick it off...

"Are you paying attention?" Nexhan asked, annoyed.

Cole blinked.

After gathering more pegs and bags, Nexhan handed them to Cole. "Let's see it."

Sighing, Cole reluctantly went to another tree. Nexhan's presence unsettled him. The Rune Fang's immense energy soaked into Cole like the summer sun and Nexhan's scent practically roared in Cole's nose. Swallowing hard, he got with the program. He used the stone to hammer the peg but ended up dropping it. He flushed, his cheeks heating.

"The bark is dense, so you have to give it a single hard hit so it lodges in. Try again." The male nodded toward the tree, his eyes fixed on Cole. "Just don't…hit your hand."

"Gee, thanks for the encouragement," Cole muttered.

He positioned the peg against the groove of the bark and made an effort to hit the peg. The tube drove through the wood and stayed there. Cole looked at Nexhan, who simply dipped his head in approval. Cole continued hammering the peg in until sap began to trickle out of the breach.

"Stop. You must stop at the first drop, else you will lose it needlessly," he explained, as Cole hastily tied the bladder to the peg.

A bead of amber sap fell into the pouch, catching the retreating light and looking like a precious jewel.

"Good." Nexhan pulled his plump lips up in a smile.

Cole looked at him closely, his own grin finding its way to his mouth. Well, at least he'd done something right. He quickly turned his attention elsewhere when something flared in the male's deep eyes, something Cole wasn't brave enough to explore yet.

"Okay. You take that side. I'll take the other," Nexhan ordered.

They labored in silence, the thumping of the stone against pegs filling out the quiet, along with a few stray birds. Cole stole a glance once in a while, admiring the way Nexhan moved. He had worked up a slight sweat, the effort of driving the pegs through the tough bark no easy thing and his body glistened in the fading light. Cole swallowed hard, his heartbeat speeding up. There was something very simple and primal about what the man was doing, as if he had seen ages long since forgotten, as if…Cole *had* seen him do this before. But, that was a ridiculous thought. He couldn't describe it, could hardly understand it, but it made him want to embrace it. He watched Nexhan carefully tie the string, the knot perfect and sturdy, so unlike Cole's bulky ties.

"Cole?" Nexhan asked.

"Huh?" He looked up into Nexhan's golden eyes as he came closer.

"All done?" Nexhan inquired, examining his work.

"Yeah," Cole shuffled around, feeling heat creep across his face. That was the second time he'd been caught staring.

"Not bad." Nexhan smiled, pleased.

That meant more to Cole than it should. "How long are we supposed to leave them here?"

"A few days. They should be ready to collect by Adam's celebration," Nexhan replied then turned to Cole and placed a palm on his shoulder.

The touched startled them both. It was a common thing for shifters to touch, to show affection, but something passed between them and Nexhan quickly withdrew his hand.

"Come."

Cole sighed and followed.

* * * *

Nexhan navigated the thick trunks of the sequoias. They hadn't walked long and he was of a mind never to stop moving, if only to keep the silence. His hand still tingled. Cole's body had felt good under his palm, a sturdy frame outlined with soft, warm skin... He really needed to stop this right now. A swirling fog of lewd thoughts consumed his mind and as hard as he tried to clear it, it persisted. Why was he so attracted to Cole? Perhaps he just hadn't been laid in so long that his desires were raging from neglect.

Regardless, it needed to stop. He'd not come home to hump the first thing he saw.

He heard the cougar trailing behind him, shuffling his feet almost in a sulking way. No wonder he'd been caught by humans. Cole made more noise than an enraged grizzly bear. Still, there was something very appealing about Cole. Not just the physical aspect, but something deep inside that called to Nexhan. And it scared him—not because he didn't know what it was, but because it seemed so familiar—a piece of a life long ago lost.

He stopped, pissed at himself for almost missing his intended location. He turned to regard the cougar-shifter, who regarded him with weariness and...heat? Yeah, Nexhan recognized that look. Guess they were both in the same tree, as it were. *Interesting*. But, that interest was quickly gone as Cole waited for him to say something, a mask of arrogant youth crossing over his face.

Nexhan set the bow and quiver down then asked, "Have you been on any of our hunts?"

Immediately, color crept up Cole's neck. He tossed his hair around. "Ah no, not exactly."

Nexhan stroked his chin. "Nakoda has told me you have not yet mastered your cat's predatory skills."

The expression Cole gave him was both anger at having pointed that out and shame from the truth. Nexhan decided not to press the point. It would get him nowhere. Cole would become defensive and quarrelsome to protect his emotions. Nexhan had recognized that defense mechanism right away. It was not unlike Nexhan's own, his vengeance masking the hurt that lay just under the surface.

He pulled out a thin leather strap from his jeans pocket then tied his hair back into a loose ponytail.

"Come here," he commanded.

Cole hesitated.

"In the old days, we would hunt using bow and arrow. Now, we use tooth and claw as they leave less evidence of our existence."

Cole furrowed his eyebrows. "Why?"

Grinning, Nexhan checked the bowstring. "We were—and are foremost—guardians, Cole. Do you know anything of our history?"

He shrugged. "No, I never really paid attention to all that history crap."

Nexhan grunted at Cole's ignorance. Such was common amongst youngsters these days and he had no idea why. Perhaps the absence of war and danger had left them bolder, naive in a way to the dark parts of the world. "Think about it. Is it not better to down your enemy from afar than up close and risk injury?"

Cole considered that for a moment. "I guess, but it's also easier that way. If you're guarding something then it makes sense to kill your enemy before they can get close."

Smiling, Nexhan traced the string with his forefinger, measuring the tightness. The cougar was smart, though he pretended not to be. "Exactly."

Nexhan watched as Cole worked the scenario over in his head.

Suspiciously, Cole asked, "What does this have to do with me?"

Nexhan didn't respond, just stood and turned to look at the cougar. Cole's stiff body language said he wanted to bolt, but pure heat resided in Cole's eyes. His sandy locks lay in wild disarray, his expression guarded. Nexhan didn't miss the way those fire-lit eyes flicked down and not at the bow as he had expected. And that gaze wasn't helping Nexhan's own attraction, either.

Cole finally got it and sputtered a laugh. "You want me to shoot that thing?"

Nexhan nodded, once.

Cole looked at him as if Nexhan's cat's pelt had gone rainbow. "You're serious?"

"Do I look like I'm joking?" It was a rhetorical question, but there was amusement in his tone.

Pursing his lips, Cole seemed unsure of what to make of the whole thing and Nexhan was of mind to seize the opportunity. So what if he did? The male was obviously in to Nexhan. It was easy to read, and Cole's scent mingled with that of attraction... Would it be so bad to sample it?

"Come here," he said, this time a little more forcefully.

Something inside him jumped when Cole obeyed. He had always been an overly dominant lover. It was just his nature and Cole's obedience enticed him further. He vaguely wondered what else the cougar might do if Nexhan commanded it.

Cole looked at him suspiciously. Nexhan handed the bow to Cole, who took it and weighed it in his hands, admiring the craftsmanship. Someone had carved images of stags into the grip, the essence of a hunt, then polished it with an enchanted varnish made from sequoia sap and a long-lost plant no longer found upon the earth.

"Its name is *Akumai'ai*, the Heart Seeker. It is willow wood taken from the trees of Shairobi. It was my father's and his father's before him. It was a gift from a Fenrir," Nexhan explained, something deep inside him hurting as memories swirled in front of him. It seemed as if it were only yesterday when he was just a cub and his father had taken him into the woods to teach him how to handle a bow. But that had been nearly seven-hundred years ago. And it seemed only last night that his father had used the bow to defend the clan, falling with *Akumai'ai* clutched in his bloody fingers.

Cole shot his eyebrows up in disbelief. "But, the wolves are…no more."

"It's true the last of their kind perished many years ago, but *Akumai'ai* has been in my family for thousands of years." Nexhan smiled, the sight of Cole holding the bow pleasing to him. Yet, he didn't know why. "The wolves and the Rune Fang were once very close. We were the guardians, they the hunters, and together we protected the Mother Goddess' domain as well as the gates."

Cole bit his lip, tracing the carvings of the stag, his eyebrows pulling down. "I didn't know that."

"Did you pay attention to anything?" Nexhan shook his head. "Do you know what the cougars once were?"

Cole blinked at him. "My father mentioned we used to be much like you. But that was a long time ago."

"He speaks the truth. Cougars were the personal guards of the Mother Goddess," Nexhan said. "Since we've left Shairobi and came to earth, much of the magic was left behind. Through both evolution and the need to adapt to this new planet, cougars and many other shifters have changed."

"Really?" Cole looked exasperated.

"Much of shifter history has been lost through the ages, but as guardians of Shairobi, we were able to preserve many tomes of knowledge that have allowed us to keep a stronger grip on the magic." He smiled, glad to see Cole interested. It was sad that many cubs did not know their own history.

"Come," Nexhan commanded.

Cole swallowed hard and looked at the bow as if it were a vicious rattlesnake.

Nexhan made his way over to the tree and drew several circles upon it with a piece of chalk. He returned and took the bow back, feeling a slight tingle against his skin. It was the magic of the bow, for *Akumai'ai* was not just a piece of weaponry but an artifact filled with potent magic. "Stand back and watch closely."

He took his spot and rolled his shoulders before righting his spine and notching an arrow. He hitched the bow up and aimed for the center of the circles. He took a deep breath, held it for a moment then let the projectile fly. The arrow hit dead center, making a thunk as it drove through the bark. He turned to regard Cole with a grin. "I have not fired a bow for many years. But it's as they say—once you learn to ride a bike, you never really forget."

Cole slumped his shoulders.

"Come try." Nexhan offered him the bow.

Cole took it reluctantly, weighing it, then looked at Nexhan who nodded toward the bullseye. Nexhan stepped back and watched as Cole retrieved an arrow from the quiver and notched it. His stance was all wrong, his body too tight, but Nexhan let the male try it.

Pulling the string, Cole held it then let it go. The projectile cut the air and dug into the bark of the redwood, but he had missed the outermost circle by a good two feet. Cole cursed something inventive that not even Nexhan had heard in his one hundred years among the human population.

"No one masters anything on the first try," Nexhan tried to soothe.

"Yeah, right. I wasn't even close." Cole huffed.

"I did not even hit the tree my first time." Nexhan smiled tightly, not liking to admit that.

Cole quieted. "Really?"

"I do not make it a habit to lie," he replied. "As embarrassing as it is, it is truth."

That seemed to sober the cougar-shifter and he looked at the bow then to the target as if he wanted to give it another go. He closed his eyes tightly for a second then reached for another arrow. Nexhan approached him silently, his bare feet making no sound. He came up behind Cole and the male stiffened.

"Relax. You're too tense. Widen your feet," he said, using his foot to pry Cole's legs apart. Nexhan dragged a hand up his spine slowly. "Stand erect."

That only succeeded in making Cole stiffen more, so Nexhan rubbed his shoulders, using the whole thing as an excuse to touch the man. His modern T-shirt was warm from his body heat and Nexhan dearly wished

Cole was shirtless. Eventually, the cougar began to relax as Nexhan sent positive waves of energy into him. Nexhan came closer, his lips but an inch from Cole's ear, that heady, sweet scent permeating his nose as he urged Cole into firing position.

"Just don't see the target. Imagine it. Will the arrow to go where you want it to go. That is part of the magic of *Akumai'ai*," Nexhan whispered.

Cole swallowed hard, his throat shifting almost provocatively, as if daring Nexhan to steal a taste.

Nexhan stepped back, giving the cougar room to breathe and concentrate on the task. Cole positioned himself and aimed, his bottom lip going in between his teeth. He pulled the string, his focus completely on the target. A moment of silence followed, as if time had stopped for a fraction of a second, then he let the arrow fly. The projectile cut the air and slammed into the bark an inch from Nexhan's own.

Cole hissed and barked a curse, dropping the bow. Nexhan's superior reflexes kicked in, his muscles springing into action and he caught *Akumai'ai* just before it would have hit the ground. He glared up at the cougar, but he sobered as Cole shook his hand in the air.

"It stung me…or something," he said, looking at the palm of his hand.

"What?" Nexhan slung *Akumai'ai* over his shoulder where it would be safe and roughly took Cole's hand in his, still a bit pissed that his father's bow had been treated so carelessly. "I don't see anything." Then he ran his fingers over Cole's skin. It was smooth and warm, not from body heat but from magic, as if he'd had a firm grip on potent energy for a long time. He looked up to regard Cole and smiled. "*Akumai'ai* has recognized you."

"Huh?" Cole blinked at him, his lips parting, his breath picking up.

Nexhan let him go reluctantly. "What is your name?"

Cole looked at him puzzled "Um?"

"Your family name," Nexhan clarified, squinting at the male.

"Nicoyla. Why?" He rubbed his palm.

Nexhan thought for a moment. "That is an old name."

"Okay?" Cole frowned.

"Nicoyla was one of the original family lines originating from Shairobi, our home land," Nexhan said, but the expression on the cougar's face made him feel as if he was trying to explain trigonometry.

"I think my dad mentioned something about that," Cole muttered, running his fingers through his locks. Nexhan noted Cole had a habit of doing that when unsure of something.

A slow grin curled over Cole's lips when he looked at the tree. "Hey, guess I didn't do too bad?"

"No, not bad at all," Nexhan sighed to himself and looked up toward the canopy of trees. The light was fading, but they still had some time. *Thank the Goddess for summer hours.* "Come."

Cole didn't ask where they were going, just followed obediently, but Nexhan felt the male's curiosity, knew he wanted to ask more about the bow. Nexhan was a bit curious about the whole ordeal as well. *Akumai'ai* had not recognized anyone for a very long time... In fact, the last time had been when his father had placed it in his hands. And even if one were of old blood, the artifact was not guaranteed to warm to their touch. So what did that mean? Nexhan had always assumed the bow had touched him because he was clan leader...

He'd ask Nakoda about that later. The man was a scholar of sorts, a lot of his free time spent on the scrolls they kept safe. Most of Nexhan's knowledge had come from his father's words and a few less-than-enthusiastic trips to their treasury to study the literature. He chuckled to himself. He wasn't that different from the young cougar, was he?

An energy wave caught his attention, the disturbance in the air so minute he had nearly missed it. He stopped, perked his ears and pulled the cooling air deep into his lungs.

"What?"

Nexhan held up his hand to silence Cole then took the cougar's palm in his. That tingle he got whenever touching the male quickly slinked its way up his arm like the kiss of a lightning bolt. He settled Cole's hand against the rough bark of a sequoia and whispered, "Feel not with your body but with your soul."

Knitting his eyebrows in confusion, Cole tried to focus. Then his expression quickly changed from one of disbelief to that of amazement. Nexhan knew what he was feeling. The earth was speaking to him through a medium.

"What do you hear?" he whispered.

Cole moved his mouth silently for a few moments before finally finding his voice. "Deer?"

Nexhan smiled then pointed over to the brush, a little surprised the inexperienced cougar had gotten it right. They took up cover on top of a fallen sequoia, their perch allowing them a slightly better view. The felled tree rested between two other redwoods so the deer were cloaked by both tree and height.

Nexhan pressed his finger against his lips then slowly, carefully, pulled *Akumai'ai* from his shoulder. Cole watched him intently. Nexhan retrieved an arrow from the quiver then pretended to be invisible. He had essentially become one with the tree, his bare feet hard against the mossy bark, his breath calm and soft, as if it were nothing more than a natural breeze traveling the forest.

Cole shifted around a bit. Nexhan saw him blink at him out of his peripheral vision, move around again and unsettle the tiny foliage on the felled tree. Nexhan placed a big hand on Cole's thigh in an attempt to get him to relax. Nexhan was focused on his task, though, and refused to let that touch arouse him.

A red deer made an appearance, its regally antlered head swiveling around, its nostrils flaring as it carefully navigated the ground. They were far enough away and shaded by tree and leaf that they weren't so obvious to the skittish creature, but the beast jerked as Cole made sounds he probably wasn't aware he was making. Nexhan got the impression he wanted to crouch, a cat instinct. Not surprising, considering this was probably Cole's first hunt in his human form.

The stag lowered its head and began pulling at the grasses.

Nexhan squeezed the cougar's thigh. Cole's attention shot to him. Nexhan leaned in and whispered softly, Cole's sharp hearing allowing him to hear every word.

"Visualize where you want the arrow to go." Then Nexhan handed *Akumai'ai* to him.

"What?" Cole whispered harshly, shaking his head.

The stag flinched and perked its ears. Cole held his breath, and when the deer returned to feeding, he said, "I can't."

"How do you know you can't if you've never tried?" Nexhan reasoned. Sure, he wasn't good with his cat, but he had proved he had some skill with a bow. Nexhan inclined his head toward the deer.

Cole looked down for a few long moments, his throat shifting as he swallowed his nerves. Silently, he took the bow and the arrow and gently notched it, trying to be stealthy. He was a little shaky but let it fly. The string skimmed his forearm and the arrow shot into the air clumsily. The deer bolted as the projectile swiveled, bouncing off a tree and buried itself in the dirt.

Cole cursed and all but tossed *Akumai'ai* back to Nexhan. "This is stupid!"

"A deer is a completely different target than a tree," Nexhan reassured, a little confused as to how Cole could have missed so badly. He had shown excellent marksmanship skills earlier.

Cole jumped off the felled tree and stomped his feet, kicking dirt and debris. "I suck!"

"A deer is much smaller and not static like—"

"It didn't move! Stop trying to sugarcoat the truth!" Cole growled.

Nexhan shut his jaw because the male was right. He was usually not one to add fluff to the hard reality of such things, but he found himself wanting to ease Cole. He gritted his teeth and stared at the arrow for a few long seconds then moved to retrieve it as Cole cursed and spat.

"This whole thing was pointless. I can't do..." He snarled, his expression twisting with emotion.

Nexhan began to understand Cole's situation a little better as Cole punched the tree closest to him. The thing did not budge and in fact, bit him back, the rough bark splitting Cole's knuckles. That didn't seem to stop his tantrum as he looked at his bloody hand and hissed viciously.

"Calm yourself," Nexhan said softly, setting *Akumai'ai* against a tree.

Cole glared at him, his eyes dark and shiny with anger and shame. The negative waves of energy soaked into Nexhan, disheartening him. Cole was suffering, albeit silently. Nexhan felt the male's pain almost as if it were his own. He knew what it was like wanting to run from the pain rather than face it. That was a bit surprising, considering the cougar wasn't a part of the clan, nor were he and Cole close.

"Cole," Nexhan growled sternly.

The male spun around and snapped. "What!"

"Yelling and hitting things will not solve the problem," he stated, placing the arrow into the quiver.

Cole quieted and studied Nexhan for a second. He dropped his attention to his hand, flexing his fingers. "No, but it sure makes me feel better." Then he looked at the tree as if he wanted to hit it again.

Nexhan decided to take action and strode toward the cougar before he could bloody any more knuckles. He took Cole's hand in his and surveyed the damage. It was slight and would heal up completely in a day or two, depending on how strong his blood was.

"I understand your frustration. I really do. But injuring yourself will not help. If a weapon is broken, then it cannot be used," Nexhan said, running his fingers along the shifter's own, testing for any cracked bones.

He heard Cole grunt in disbelief and mutter something about how he was like an eternally blunt blade — or something along those lines. The male was ready to bolt. Nexhan could feel it in the tenseness of Cole's body, see it in his stance. So, he brought the cougar's hand to his lips. He wasn't sure why he did, since the wound was not so bad that it needed attention, but it was as if his body was acting of its own accord.

Cole gasped as Nexhan curled his tongue over Cole's knuckles, lapping up the blood and sealing the cuts with his saliva. The taste of the young male's blood was exquisite on his tongue, like the sweet, thick sap of the sequoias but with a hearty spice. When there was no more blood, he didn't stop. It was not uncommon for shifters to lick each other's wounds. Their saliva held healing properties and it was often done to show affection and concern, but his actions were quickly approaching lewdness. Realizing what he was doing, he let go of the cougar's hand abruptly.

Cole's lips were parted and moist, his lids low, the sandy fringe of his lashes shrouding his dilated pupils. A healthy glow highlighted his skin. When his scent hit Nexhan... *Oh, Goddess.* The pheromones crashed into him like a brick wall and permeated deep inside him, awaking his entire body. Cole wanted him. Desperately.

Nexhan cleared his throat. "Forgive me. I should have asked permission." That was probably a stupid thing to say. Affection was freely given and, in turn, freely accepted. Perhaps, he had spent too long among the humans. Their way of thinking must have changed his own.

Confused, the male flinched his eyebrows downward for a moment but he never lost that heated look. Nexhan knew he should step away, but he couldn't. His arousal pressed against the fly of his pants. He wanted to let it out and get closer to Cole. Cole locked his eyes on him like two powerful magnets, pulling Nexhan in. It had been too long since he'd felt another body against his in a sexual way and he was desperate for it.

Cole raised his injured hand and took a lock of Nexhan's hair that had come loose. He played with it for a moment, admiring the softness, then brought it to his nose. He inhaled deeply, his intense eyes flicking to Nexhan's lips in a silent demand. It was at that moment that Nexhan realized he had seriously underestimated this man, for Cole *was* a man and not a kid. Though he was young, he was still a full-grown shifter, a sexual creature with primal desires. His body was eager and ready. It was strong and muscled, moist with perspiration and eager to be used. Nexhan didn't need to look down to know Cole was sporting a matching hard-on.

Tossing all his inhibitions to the wild wind, Nexhan stepped forward. Cole didn't budge, and when they were but an inch from each other, Cole—not Nexhan—made the first move. Cole pressed his lips against Nexhan's, sweeping his tongue over the seam of Nexhan's mouth, searching for a way in, his need evident. Nexhan gave him more, wrapping his arm around Cole's back, and digging his fingers into the male's ass. He pressed his body against Cole's, their cocks meeting through their clothes. Cole gasped and Nexhan took over the kiss. He was going to make one thing clear—he was the top cat, as it were. He was dominant to the core and would control how it was going to go down.

Cole was clearly on board with the plan, letting his hands go in Nexhan's hair, pulling the tie loose as they sucked at each other's mouths. Cole moaned against Nexhan's lips as Nexhan drove deeper into him, demanding more, their tongues entwining furiously.

Cole gave in as Nexhan backed him up against the tree Cole had assaulted. Nexhan was none too gentle as he whipped the male's T-shirt over Cole's head and tossed it away. Cole looked to the side, offering his neck, as though sensing how badly Nexhan had wanted to taste that enticing piece of flesh. Nexhan didn't hesitate. He flattened his tongue against Cole's skin and dragged it upward and across the hard line of Cole's jaw. Cole groaned and bucked against Nexhan's hips, stroking both their cocks. Nexhan licked his way into the male's mouth languorously, the kiss much gentler.

Nexhan had always had a habit of kissing with his eyes open. It was so much more fun that way, being able to watch the expression on his lover's face. Cole was truly beautiful. His eyelashes lay tight against his cheeks, his brows pulling down in a mask of agonized pleasure. This close, Nexhan could see the light spattering of freckles on Cole's cheeks. The male's fangs had come down slightly through his parted lips, the passion surging through him waking that raw, ancient instinct. Shifters retained a part of their animal halves while in human form, such as fangs, enhanced senses. Then, while in their animal bodies, they held on to their higher thought processes and emotions.

The sound that Cole made as Nexhan gripped Cole's cock through his pants was all animal. "Fuck me. Please...fuck me."

Nexhan hushed him and flicked his tongue across Cole's jaw, slowly making his way back down Cole's neck, leaving a trail of soft nips and rough kisses. Cole curled his fingers tightly in Nexhan's hair as Nexhan moved south, where he sucked Cole's erect nipple into his mouth. Cole hissed and arched into him as Nexhan teased the point with his teeth, biting gently while tracing the subtle slopes of Cole's abs. Nexhan pulled with his lips and scraped with his teeth until Cole writhed above him.

Nexhan came back up to his full height and undid the button to his own jeans then pulled down the zipper of his fly. He leaned in against Cole's ear and purred, "You want me to fuck you?"

"Please," Cole growled hoarsely.

"Then get me ready," Nexhan demanded.

Cole didn't waste a second, dropping to his knees and shucking Nexhan's pants down his thighs. Nexhan's cock popped out, a long, thick shaft weeping at the tip. Nexhan savored the sight of Cole devouring him urgently, those lips stretching to take in all he could. Nexhan buried his fingers in the male's hair, wishing he had some support at his back. He was wobbly from the intense emotions roiling through him, the pleasure making his limbs weak.

Cole made little mewls of pleasure as he sucked Nexhan off, deep and fast, his hands firmly on Nexhan's ass, demanding more, and Nexhan found himself rocking against his lover's mouth. He knew he was big, but Cole took it all and that aroused Nexhan like nothing else. It wasn't long before his balls tightened, his skin gleaming with sweat. He had become oversensitive, the very breeze like a third body against his. As intriguing as it was to come in Cole's mouth, he wanted to feel the male's body under him, wanted to experience Cole's ass grasping his cock as he drove into him over and over.

"That's enough," Nexhan ground out and tugged at Cole's hair aggressively.

Chapter Five

Nexhan spun Cole around so fast that Cole was sure his brain had jostled inside his skull, but he didn't care. In fact, he wanted more. Nexhan was on him in an instant, the male's muscular chest plastered against Cole's back as Nexhan pressed him down onto the earth. Cole surprised himself with the half-sigh, half-moan that escaped his lips. He had wanted this so bad for too long. Well, he'd actually only known the shifter for two days, but it felt like so much longer than that. Then again, when one yearned for something and didn't get it, every minute seemed like an eternity.

Nexhan's salty taste remained on his tongue. Cole had wanted to bring Nexhan to climax that way, wanted to feel all that wet warmth slide down his throat, but he understood clearly that Nexhan was in charge—and that was just fine with Cole as long as Nexhan didn't stop what he was doing.

Nexhan lowered his mouth to Cole's back, planting tantalizing little kisses as he shrugged Cole's jeans down his hips. Cole gave in to the man, letting him do what he wanted, submitting completely. Strong hands roamed his body, massaged his back, and gripped the globes of his ass roughly. The guy didn't waste time finding Cole's entrance. He circled the puckered opening with skill, sending a sharp chill up Cole's spine.

Cole bumped his head on the ground and groaned. Yes, this was what he wanted. Needed. *Please!*

Nexhan's voice sounded like chocolate in Cole's ear — smooth and dark. "Has anyone been here before?"

To accentuate his point, Nexhan thrust against the sensitive tissue without entering Cole but letting Cole know of his intent.

Cole could barely speak. "Humans."

"And shifter?"

Cole shook his head.

"Good," Nexhan growled. "That's good."

Cole had heard that sex with shifters was unparalleled. It was just more intense, more vibrant than with humans. But, he'd never been intimate with another shifter before, so he couldn't be sure. But what ran through him at this moment was better than anything he'd had with male humans and they hadn't even gotten to the fucking part yet. He wanted — needed — more. It was as if he did this with Nexhan then he'd be more...more shifter, a better male, just more everything.

Nexhan pressed him face down against the turf so that Cole could feel every rippling muscle against his back. The heat of the evening, the work and the passion slicked their bodies with sweat. With his soft lips, Nexhan kissed Cole's shoulder, creating a gentle suction, but Nexhan pulled, effectively marking him. Cole bit his lip. He was monstrously hard, the earth cool against the heat of his skin.

Nexhan retreated and Cole craned his neck to see what the holdup was. The male whispered words of magic in a tongue that seemed vaguely familiar then traced something on the base of the redwood with his fingertip. Golden sap oozed out from between the grooves of the bark and he took it in his palm.

Playfulness engulfed Cole and he teased, "If you could draw forth sap that easily, why did we go through all that work earlier?"

"Manual labor is good for you," Nexhan said, his voice husky.

There was more than one meaning to his words and Cole got it loud and clear. Nexhan was going to work him out good, especially as the Rune Fang spread Cole's ass cheeks and smeared the cool, sticky sap up and down Cole's crack. Soothing. Cole relaxed against the forest floor. It wasn't like he could do much of anything else with all that weight and demand up against his body. That realization made him hotter and the pulsing in his cock matched the thump of his heart.

Nexhan's fingers were gentle and smooth as he prodded, slipping one into Cole's passage. Cole groaned, digging his fingers into the dirt and plant debris. The man's lips returned to his shoulder, kissing tenderly, licking slyly. Nexhan's hair had fallen free, the locks spilling over in a blanket of dark blue silk. '*More*', Cole wanted to say, but his parched throat kept him from speaking. He was being teased, that single finger stroking the fire inside him, making him burn with no relief in sight. But Nexhan retreated and Cole growled, the sound animalistic. He was a slave to his own needs.

Nexhan chuckled darkly and pressed his cock against Cole's ass. That shut him up, but he couldn't help arching, pleading for more stimulation. He wanted to feel that tool stretching him like it had his mouth, the heavily veined shaft stroking him deep inside. Nexhan wrapped an arm around Cole's waist, pulling Cole snugly against him then thrusting. Cole gasped at the intrusion, the massive erection spreading him to the max. There was pain, but only at first, then a colossal explosion of pleasure as Nexhan's cock drove into him all the way to the hilt. Cole bit down on his bottom lip until he tasted blood, trying to quell the quakes running through his body.

Nexhan chuckled as Cole came. *Shit.* He had never come like this before and definitely not so quickly. Damn, it felt good. If this was what it was like to have sex with another shifter, he wasn't sure he could survive the demand that was Nexhan. But fuck, he wanted to try.

The Rune Fang held him close, planting sweet little kisses against Cole's back, Nexhan's cock twitching inside Cole's ass. Cole liked the primal power up against him, the loss of control, everything. Then Nexhan began to move and it was…indescribable. Sensations broke over Cole's skin, the warmth of the air and the light tickling of the breeze enhancing the feeling. The earth below him grew cooler, softer, cushioning him as the hardness above drilled into him. He dug his fingers deeper into the soil and it was as if the earth was holding him, the soil wrapping its grainy fingers around his so that he couldn't move. All he could do was…accept.

His lungs ached as he struggled to breathe and his throat protested as he groaned against the pounding. Nexhan's balls slapped against Cole's and his teeth dug into Cole's skin. The male was raw natural power unleashed like the wild ocean, and Cole was the shorebeing battered, bearing the blunt of the force. It all seemed so right, so perfectly natural.

Nexhan suddenly slowed his thrusts, lessened his depth and whispered against Cole's ear. There was a hint of astonishment to his tone. "Look."

Delirious from the pleasure, all Cole could do was blink. He felt Nexhan curling his fingers in his hair then tugging lightly, forcing him to look up. Spring grass surrounded them like a gentle, green blanket. Stems of various flowers and plants uncurled, leaves unfolded and grew in front of their very eyes. The new life slowly spread outward, turning the barren clearing into a grove.

"W-what's happening?" Cole managed to ask.

Nexhan simply laughed, a booming, cheerful sound, full of life. Then he resumed his thrusting and Cole growled loudly, his balls tightening, preparing to shoot off another load. Nexhan reached around and grab Cole's dick snugly and began stroking him. Every time the man hit the sensitized head of his cock, Cole flinched in pleasure. Nexhan widened his knees, the width of his body forcing Cole to comply. Nexhan drew deeper into him, his breath hitching, his soft grunts intensifying.

Cole was able to look up toward the spreading foliage then he knew rapture and ecstasy and life as his entire body exploded in bliss, the intense waves of the orgasm rippling through him like an aftershock. The growing blanket of life hastened and touched the redwoods. The moss on the bark thickened and there the scent of flowers on the wind reached him as Nexhan pounded into him, snarling something vicious into the air as he released his load into Cole.

A warmth spread through Cole, if that was even possible. It was like his own personal sun had been beating down on him all day, his skin on fire and the wave of heat roiled through him, igniting his insides as he shuddered with the waves of the orgasm. Colors bloomed before Cole's eyes—red like blood, blue as the morning sky, soft buttery yellow like the autumn wheat. He was aware he was voicing his pleasure rather loudly, but he couldn't help it. It just went on and on until Nexhan collapsed against him, the shock of his weight breaking the spell. Cole lay with his cheek against the grass, and he huffed, trying to recover from the blowout, trying to regain a semblance of higher thinking.

Nexhan's hot breath blew against Cole's neck then the light press of Nexhan's lips followed on his shoulder. The male glided his palm across Cole's deltoid tenderly, down his arm, all rough intentions gone from his touch. Nexhan found Cole's fingers in the soil and slowly pried them loose, wrapping his hand around them. He planted sweet kisses against Cole's back as Cole finally began to come down from the high.

Nexhan whispered in his ear, "Are you okay?"

Weakly, Cole nodded. "That was... It was... I..."

The Rune Fang exhaled on a chuckle. "You cannot find with a human what you can find with me."

Cole grinned. He could say that again.

Sighing with pleasure, Nexhan slowly pulled out of Cole and coaxed him to join him on the new grass. Cole rolled around and snuggled up against Nexhan's bigger body, the male's chest a rather comfortable pillow for the size and hardness. Nexhan wrapped an arm around him, hugging him close and Cole couldn't help hooking a finger around the long satin locks that streamed across Nexhan's chest. Utterly exhausted and completely satisfied, he smiled until his cheeks hurt.

A new scent caught their attention and they both looked to the side and watched as a single white rose bloomed against a thorny bush. Cole got closer to Nexhan so that he could see the male's face. Nexhan looked at him, his luminous eyes glittering with satisfaction. The harsh planes of his perfectly sculpted face had softened, his lips in a peaceful smile.

"What's going on?" Cole asked.

The look that crossed Nexhan's face told him he wasn't entirely sure, but he answered, "It is a blessing from the Mother."

Whatever that means. Honestly, it was a little creepy, but he was in too good of a mood to allow it bother him, so he let it pass and lay his head back down against Nexhan, reveling in the closeness. This was what he had wanted for the longest time, only he'd been too afraid to reach out and snag it. He'd closed himself off from his clan, had run from his fears, but now... He closed his eyes tightly, losing himself in the presence of his lover.

Nexhan shifted so that they were lying on their sides, facing each another. Nexhan ran his fingers across his back lovingly. Every shifter craved touch, whether sexual or just for comfort, but Cole realized at this moment just how far apart he had grown, not just from his clan but also from who he was. Despite his inadequacies, he was still shifter. There was something to be said about being naked on the grass with the light fading at his back and the warmth of another next to him. And lying here with Nexhan, after experiencing one of the greatest joys the Mother Goddess had gifted them with, among all the new growth... *I feel complete.*

Cole took a deep breath and held it for a few moments, the heavy scent of flowers in his lungs. He slowly let it leak from his body.

"Is there something you want to ask?" Nexhan purred.

"Yeah." He bit his lip that was sore from the earlier chewing. "I was wondering if you'd tell me about the old days. Shairobi and...stuff."

"I thought you didn't care for all that history crap?" Nexhan teased, his smile radiant.

Cole shrugged. "Curious." *I love the sound of his voice.*

The Rune Fang studied him for a few moments, his eyes alight with amusement. "There is so much to tell. Where should I begin?"

"The beginning, I guess." Cole shrugged again, resting his head against Nexhan. There was something very soothing about the man, as if his immense strength and power could keep Cole safe from anything. And his voice was so very comforting. If Cole didn't know that Nexhan was feline, he would have taken him for a big, fluffy teddy bear.

"The beginning. Okay. All shifters are the product of the union between the Mother Goddess and the Gray Man," Nexhan said, looking up into the tree's branches.

Cole closed his eyes and listened to Nexhan speak, mesmerized by the way the man enunciated his words. Nexhan's voice was a rumble in his chest and all the while, Cole thought there was no other place he'd rather be.

Chapter Six

Thunk.

Nexhan had always liked the sound of an arrow hitting wood. It reminded him of happier times.

Nexhan took a big breath and held it until his lungs began to protest. Slowly, he let the cleansing breath out. The sun had climbed high and the early morning fog had lifted, leaving the landscape clear and cloudless. It was getting hot, the midsummer weather a bit unusual in this area, but nonetheless, the clan was enjoying the day.

Nexhan's brothers and the human, Caroline, filled the bathing pool. She sat on the bank, her smooth legs in the pond. Her babe, nestled in between her thighs, splashed joyously at the water. She had on a little bikini suit that hid any hints of recent motherhood and the males all sported swim trunks. It was unusual for them to hide their nudity, but Nexhan reckoned Caroline wouldn't feel comfortable with body parts swinging around so shamelessly—it was a squeamishness that humans held and shifters lacked. It was nice to see his brothers so happy, though, with big smiles and bright eyes as they doted over Mewah's mate and cub. The last time he had seen their faces...

Faces of ash and the tears that cleaned the dust away...
Stricken expressions and moans of despair...
His own choked cry as he held Inari's cooling body...
Thunk.

Nexhan had awoken to that sound not too long ago. He had been surprised he'd slept so late, but then again, he hadn't taken much rest during the night. His tryst with Cole had been refreshing and much needed. Nexhan closed his eyes, recalling the way the cougar-shifter's skin had felt against his own and the way the male had looked caught up in the ecstasy. Then they had talked all night, gently caressing each other. Cole had seemed genuinely interested in everything he'd had to tell about their history. They had finally returned to the village before dawn and went their own separate ways, shy smiles gracing their faces.

Thunk.

Nexhan could safely say he understood the young male now. Nexhan had been away from his clan for a hundred years, and every day he'd been away, he'd craved the touch of another shifter so badly that he ached from the loneliness. To feel the heat of kin against his flesh, to let their life-force soak into him, was unlike anything else. Cole craved it too, was desperate for it, and Nexhan wondered why the cougar had isolated himself from his family. Was it because he was clumsy? He hadn't asked, though, fearing the male would close up.

Nexhan bit his lip as he watched Cole direct Cherchi to move the archery butte further. Cherchi's body shone from his exertion as he retrieved arrows and lugged the heavy object around, but he was all smiles.

From his position, Nexhan could see that Cole had gotten a good work out as well, his back glistened with a sheen of sweat, his body naked except for a pair of jean shorts. He looked as delectable as ever and Nexhan couldn't help but to remember the way he had tasted.

"He's been at it for hours now," Nakoda informed, coming up beside Nexhan. "I had no idea he was so good with a bow."

Nexhan grunted a response, filing away his lewd thoughts lest his body betray him. "I took him into the woods last eve to help me lay sap, then had him try the bow."

"Ah, so that was where you disappeared to." Nakoda smiled softly. There was something in that look that belied he knew more than Nexhan was willing to let on to.

"You covered his chores. It is only right that he do the same," Nexhan said defensively. He didn't want any of his brothers to know what was going on between them, at least not yet. Sex was not a shameful thing to be hidden, but he felt as if he shouldn't be enjoying such pleasures — as if he wasn't worthy. He'd abandoned his family, left his clan to fend for itself, all because he was a nancy and couldn't handle his emotions. He didn't deserve to know such a life when his people were teetering on the brink of extinction.

Nexhan saw Nakoda nod then sober. "I had dismissed him. When he first came to us, I had taken him with me to assist with various things, but it soon became clear that he was...inept. I see now that I had not taken the time to find his individual talents. Was that cruel of me?"

Looking into the kind eyes of his best friend, Nexhan smiled. "No."

His expression lightening, Nakoda watched as Cole shot an arrow right smack in the middle of the bullseye painted upon the haystack. Another perfect shot. "Well, I have matters to attend to, *Mi'wisa*."

"Brother?" Nexhan asked. "Will you do me a favor and scour the library for old family lines concerning the cougars?"

Nakoda looked a bit surprised. "He is old blood."

"*Akumai'ai* recognized him," Nexhan admitted. He sensed his brother's shock.

"That is...unprecedented."

"Perhaps, then again only my family line has ever handled it," he said. "It may just have recognized his bloodline and nothing more."

Nakoda seemed to mull over that for a few moments then clapped Nexhan on the shoulder, his long orange hair swaying gently in the breeze. "I shall see what I can uncover."

"Thank you." Nexhan pulled his friend in for a bear hug, aware of just how badly he had missed him. Nakoda chuckled merrily and patted him on the back, then planted a kiss on his forehead. Nexhan sighed as he watched his friend leave.

Thunk. Then a curse as Cole shook his hand in the air. Still, he had landed another flawless shot.

Nexhan grinned to himself and made his way over to Cole, as he was directing Cherchi to move the butte farther. "Cole."

Cole spun around to look at him, his mask of frustration bleeding away into joy and heat. Nexhan smirked and took the cougar's hand in his, running his fingers over the raw skin of his forearm. Cole winced.

Nexhan barked, "Cherchi, that is it for today."

"But—" Cole protested.

"Come."

A tick jumped in Cole's jaw, but he didn't say anything and followed Nexhan. When they were alone, Nexhan chuckled and threw an arm around the man's shoulders pulling him in. "Stop sulking."

Cole growled but he was all smiles. "I'm not."

"You are. I have something for you that will cheer you up, though."

"Yeah?" he said almost wistfully, those big violet marbles blinking at Nexhan with mischief and lust.

Nexhan led them to his private quarters, a small log cabin among many. He shut the door behind them and took *Akumai'ai* from Cole, settling it against the wall.

He pushed Cole playfully and the male landed on the bed, laughing. But as much as Nexhan wanted to join him, he made for a chest crafted of solid oak and carved with various animals from wolves and tigers to deer and horses. Nexhan muttered words of magic and the lock unhinged. He sifted around until he found what he was looking for then turned to Cole. He kneeled between the male's legs and the cougar shifted around, biting his lip in anticipation.

Nexhan smiled to himself and fought the urge to pin Cole between the cushions with his body. Instead, he took Cole's hand in his, running his fingers over the reddened skin of his forearm. It was already healing. In fact, it had been trying to for a while, but the repeated irritation wasn't helping. "This is a common problem."

Cole stiffened as Nexhan got closer, Cole's breathing hitching up, but, business first. He unfolded a piece of cloth, revealing a bracer. "This will help protect your arm when you fire. It was made by my great-great grandmother and carved from Totoa hide, a beast native to our homeland."

As Cole pressed his legs against Nexhan's sides, Nexhan placed the bracer on the cougar's arm and did up the leather ties. He was sure he heard Cole mutter "thanks", but he was too busy listening to the words of Cole's body. The man had grown hard and the scent of his arousal had stiffened Nexhan's own cock.

"There," Nexhan mumbled.

Cole looked at the bracer and fingered it, tracing the carvings and admiring the craftsmanship. "This is yours?"

"Was," Nexhan corrected. "Now I have no need for it. Better it go to you than collect dust in some chest."

Cole made a sound of disagreement but looked at Nexhan with wonderment and true gratitude. "Thank you. Really."

"You are welcome." Nexhan beamed then dropped his attention to Cole's hard-on. "Now, we have business to attend to."

He didn't need to say anything more. They both moved at the same time, meeting at the lips, Cole's fingers digging into his skin, trying to pull him closer. Nexhan pressed the cougar down on the bed and sank into him, feeding at his mouth. Cole growled and wrapped his legs around Nexhan's hips, and proceeded to grind his cock against Nexhan's.

Feeling voracious, Nexhan took hold of Cole's hands and pinned them above Cole's head. Cole fought against him for a few moments before finally relaxing. Nexhan closed the distance between their lips, slowly, seductively, and every time Cole would try to reach him, he'd move away. The cougar growled but he was all smiles.

"What?" Nexhan teased. The night before he'd been rough, thirsty, but now he wanted to savor.

Cole ground his hips against Nexhan in a silent plea, but wickedness filled his expression. Nexhan came to his lips gently and Cole accepted. The shifter's lips were soft, inviting and Nexhan slipped in a little tongue. He busied his free hand, spanning the length of Cole's chest, fingering his erect nipple. The sound Cole made against Nexhan's mouth caused Nexhan's cock to jump in excitement.

Nexhan released his mouth and planted light kisses along the man's jaw then down his throat. He inhaled the scent of Cole's skin, peppermint-laced with pheromones calling to him. He dragged his tongue over the sensitive flesh until he found what he wanted, curling around the hard bud.

Cole arched his back and moaned.

"Mi'wisa!" a voice called.

Nexhan jumped back and Cole shot up just as Cherchi burst through the door. He had a big smile on his face, but it faltered. No doubt the scent of arousal in the air had caught his attention.

"What is it?" Nexhan barked harshly, angry at having been interrupted.

Cherchi beamed. "We have visitors!"

As if to accentuate his point, the smooth cry of a hawk sounded in the distance. Nexhan looked at Cole, who flushed, then Nexhan grinned before breaking out in a run for the door. Cherchi laughed and ran with Nexhan. Nexhan glanced back and was pleased to see that Cole was following, albeit reluctantly.

They joined the rest of the clan under *Weynka Le Gai* and Nexhan instantly spotted the object of everyone's joy. Three huge hawks were circling the tree, their musical cries filling the air in a heavenly chorus. They were big, twice the size of normal hawks, and ranged from the color of earthen mud and rock to the deep sienna of the setting sun.

The first bird, the color of red clay and boasting a regally crested head, folded his wings and bolted down toward the earth. Nexhan roared with laughter as he ducked to avoid the hawk's playful swipe, the talons able to do extreme damage if intended. The raptor-shifter came to land, its huge wingspan twisting into a mass of feathers and color until a man stood, smiling at Nexhan with ancient, kind eyes. His skin reminded Nexhan of sun-baked clay, with hair as dark as a moonless night cascading over his shoulders. He was fair, his features sharp and angular, eyes glowing orange. The fairest of the three hawks, the color of sandstone, landed to join the man. An elegant-looking woman appeared from a burst of spectral light. They both wore soft deer hide. Beads of polished bone and stone decorated their limbs.

Nexhan beamed. "Donoma, lord of air. I greet you!"

The hawk tipped his dark head, the locks streaked with brown and accented with colorful feathers. "Nexhan, Gatekeeper, I am glad to be here."

The greeting was proper, but the formality was quickly dropped as they crashed their bodies together, patting each other on the back as they embraced. Nexhan inhaled deeply, sucking the hawk's breezy scent into his lungs.

Donoma laughed merrily. "It has been too long, my friend."

Nexhan held him at arm's length and smiled ruefully for a moment. "Indeed it has."

He turned to regard the female, her smile as radiant as the morning sun. Waves of buttery highlights framed a gentle face, and bright yellow eyes radiated warmth.

He took her hand and kissed it in respect. "Chalena, as always, your light outshines the sun."

Her laughter sounded like a bird's song. "You are ever the flatterer."

"No, just the truth-speaker." He winked.

The remaining hawk joined them and Nexhan recognized Donoma's brother, Kawiinok. His expression was as Nexhan had remembered—bored yellow eyes set against tawny skin, his rich muddy hair left loose over his shoulders. The two shared rounds of hugs. It had been a long time since Nexhan had seen the hawks, his travels among the human population keeping him far from his old friends. It was a breath of fresh air to look upon them now.

A cry sounded from the branches of *Weynka Le Gai* and Nexhan spotted a very large, very black harpy eagle. It must have landed there before Nexhan had emerged from his cabin. The shifter screeched, bobbling its crested head in excitement, the show almost bordering on obnoxiousness. The eagles were few, and most tended to take up residence with the hawk clans. This one seemed intent on making its presence known.

Centuries ago, the eagles had been much more plentiful and the humans who were lucky enough to see an eagle-shifter wrote tales of the great beasts. They called them griffons. In Shairobi, the eagles had been the Mother Goddess' messengers, carrying her words across the cosmos to where the Gray Man made his home. It was truly an honor to look upon the eagle.

Donoma chuckled darkly. "And this is the fourth member of our party."

The eagle took to the sky, joining the last hawk, its looping cry suddenly like amused giggles. The shifter landed, twisting his form in a burst of blinding light, catching Nexhan off guard. The male appeared as tall as Nexhan, and his stark black hair, twisted into tiny braids, coiled around his body. Eyes as icy as the coldest northern wind seemed almost silver but that wasn't what caught Nexhan's attention. It was his urban clothing. His black leather pants hugged shapely legs and the long suede overcoat framed broad shoulders. Metal chains and beads clinked around his neck and he had several face piercings. The eagle grinned darkly.

Donoma spoke up. "This is Talon."

"Tah-lawn! I love the way you say my name with such elegance! Makes me feel important!" Talon laughed and fanned at his face, as though he were blushing.

"Talon has been visiting our nest for a few weeks now." Donoma smiled warmly. "He has adopted the way of humanity but we appreciate him nonetheless."

Chuckling, Talon pulled Nexhan in with an arm around his shoulders and whispered loudly so that all could hear, despite his intentions to keep his words private. "What he really means to say is that they think I'm coo-coo." He winked.

Nexhan didn't know what to say. He wanted to be polite and refute the raptor's words, but he agreed. This eagle was a strange one. "Welcome to our village—and you *are* welcome. It's not every day we are graced with the presence of the Messengers."

Talon grinned, poking at Nexhan's chest. "I'd say the same thing of you. Y'all are somewhat of a legend." He made a noise of excitement and pumped his fist in the air. "I come bearing gifts."

Enthusiasm quickly replaced Nexhan's confusion. A quiet cheer went up and Talon produced a backpack. He dug into it and withdrew a jar containing golden gel. The scent of real maple syrup caught Nexhan's nose and he beamed as he accepted the offering.

"Yum," Talon commented absently. He gasped and tossed some sort of tin can to the crowd. Cherchi caught and opened it.

"Slim Jims. Double yum." Talon licked his lips. "Where is it? Oh, got it! Where are we?" he said, looking around. He made another squeak then tossed a book to Nakoda. "That's from Donoma. You really into that chick porn, man? I mean…Nora Roberts?"

Nakoda smiled bashfully, his cheeks pinkening and he hid the book behind his back. "I uh… I find her stories appealing… Thank you, Donoma."

Donoma tipped his head.

Ignoring him, Talon reached into his bag. "Gawd! I feel like Santa *Claws*! Oh, here we are!"

"There's more?" Nexhan blinked, astonished.

"You betcher buns." The eagle smirked.

Donoma chuckled, truly pleased but obviously not surprised. Apparently, the hawks had grown used to the eagle's antics. "Talon has a very useful talent of being able to transport many things between forms."

"Indeed," Nexhan whispered, as Talon withdrew a brown sack that smelled sweet.

Hihano gasped in delight and the eagle tossed the sack to him. Whispers of "What is it?" bounced around the crowd.

Hihano smiled, tasting the bag's contents with his fingers. "Cocoa powder."

"Ah, and finally!" Talon gasped and pulled out a beautifully woven blanket. "Where's the lucky daddy?"

Mewah stepped forward. "I guess that's me."

Holding the gift up, Talon grinned. "On behalf of my feathered friends, I present this to you."

Mewah graciously accepted the baby blanket woven from super soft Totoa hair. Sections of the strands had been dyed in earth tones and shades of green so that when woven, a great flowering tree stretched across the blanket. Nexhan smiled warmly as Mewah thanked the raptors, tears shimmering in his eyes.

"Thank you for your gifts. I'm sure Mewah's mate will cherish the blanket," Nexhan said.

"It is not every day a guardian is born. We are thrilled to bear witness to his welcoming," Donoma beamed.

"Yes, yes, we're all excited!" Talon agreed then turned his gaze to the side. His eyes darkened slightly as if he had spotted some delicious morsel scurrying on the ground, unaware of the predator above.

Nexhan followed the eagle's gaze and Cole glared right back at Talon. Nexhan didn't like the way the shifter was looking at Cole—he wasn't sure why. Nexhan cleared his throat. "This is Cole Nicoyla of the cougars. He has been staying with us for some time now."

"Ah, yes." Donoma came forward. "We met the cougars' emissary, Kale, on the way here. He should be arriving shortly."

Nexhan heard Cole make a disrespectful noise but ignored it and turned to Nakoda. "Will you show our guests a room? And prepare one for the arriving cougar as well. Perhaps Cole would like to share his quarters with..." When Nexhan looked to where Cole was, he was gone. *Huh?*

Nakoda dipped is head respectfully and led the raptors away. Nexhan looked for Cole, but he had suddenly disappeared. Nexhan had thought the cougar would be delighted to see one of his clan brothers again, but that was obviously not the case. The crowd dispersed, many following the hawks, eager to hear stories. Nexhan spotted Cole making his way toward the forest.

Torn, Nexhan wanted to spend time with the hawks. He had not seen Donoma for a very long time and he was desperate to share stories and comforts with the male. Something pulled him toward Cole, though, like they were attached. He also sensed something was bothering the cougar.

Nexhan glanced back and forth between the village and the forest.

* * * *

Both angry and hopeful, Cole stood naked in the middle of the grove. He didn't want his brother here, didn't want to listen to the male list all the reasons why he needed to come home, and he especially didn't want Kale to get the idea that he was a lover of males. He could just picture the disappointment crossing his parents' faces at that juicy little nugget.

And he was horny, damn it. He had purposely rubbed up against the trees, leaving a trail of pheromones for Nexhan to follow — if he decided to come. Cole hoped he would. He wanted to finish what they had started on Nexhan's bed and he needed to feel that closeness they'd shared last night. He knew he was being selfish. Nexhan had obviously been ecstatic to see the hawks. What right did Cole have to demand the male spend his time with him and not his friends?

None. Stop being a selfish, demanding bitch!

Cole sighed as the cool grass tickled his feet. The vines and flowers leaned toward him as if he were a central point of attraction, and the scents of wild flowers and roses intensified. The minute energy waves of the thousands of microorganisms in the soil reached and penetrated him. The grove was awakening again, as if it had only been asleep, taking a reverie to prepare for further expansion. He'd never heard of such growth before and he wasn't sure what it meant. Neither did Nexhan apparently, his gift-from-the-Mother explanation doing little to convince Cole.

Cole inhaled the varying scents and let his breath go slowly. He wanted to feel Nexhan against him almost as badly as he needed the air in his lungs. When a heady scent caught his attention, he grinned from ear to ear, his tummy doing a tumble of excitement.

He said coolly, "It has stopped growing."

When Nexhan's encompassed Cole in his warm, strong arms, Cole fell back against Nexhan's sturdy body. Nexhan's voice coiled lazily in his ear. "I think we can fix that."

Cole smiled, resting his head against Nexhan's shoulder. He was naked, that big hard body stark against Cole's. And Nexhan was aroused. Well, wasn't that just dandy? The man placed a gentle kiss on Cole's neck and inhaled deeply while he let his hands roam Cole's midsection. Those crafty fingers gripped his dick snugly. Fangs scraped at Cole's neck. Cole groaned and dug his fingers into Nexhan's hips, absorbing the way the Rune Fang's erection felt against the crack of his ass. With his free hand, Nexhan pinched Cole's nipple. Cole arched against his lover.

Nexhan purred in his ear. "Why did you run away?"

Cole wasn't in the mood to talk about it. He wanted to fuck and he let Nexhan know with a frustrated little growl when the male stopped stroking him. Nexhan pinched his nipple again, this time harder, and Cole gasped at the pleasure-pain.

"Tell me," Nexhan growled, his tone a curl of seduction. "Or I'll stop."

Well, wasn't that a hell of an incentive? Nexhan's nails bit into Cole's sensitive flesh, stinging him, but there was also an immense pleasure building from it. Did he want Nexhan to stop? Did he want more? He wasn't entirely sure.

To accentuate his point, Nexhan lessened the pressure.

"Kale is my brood-brother," Cole bit out. He felt the Rune Fang's surprise. *Well, I guess that answers his question.*

Nexhan began stroking him tortuously slow and resumed pinching Cole's tender bud.

"And this is a problem because...?" he asked.

Cole didn't want to talk. He wanted action. No words. No opening of mouths unless it was to lick or suck something. He turned around to face the man and peered into the Rune Fang's golden eyes for a moment. There was curiosity there, but it was foreshadowed by immense lust. Cole smirked and took Nexhan's nipple in his lips, using his teeth to pull gently. The male hissed and fisted his hand in Cole's hair.

Cole nipped at the succulent flesh with his teeth and swirled his tongue, slowly falling to his knees. He tasted salt and spice as he flattened his tongue against Nexhan's abs. He looked up. Nexhan watched him carefully, his lips slightly parted, eyes dilated with arousal. Cole gripped Nexhan's balls and ran the tip of his tongue down the hard shaft.

Nexhan growled like a feral cat, clawing Cole's scalp. Cole inhaled the Rune Fang's sultry scent, branding himself with the memory, and submitted himself at Nexhan's feet as he pressed his lips against his balls. Cole slicked them up, nipped gently and flicked his tongue. Nexhan's breathing had grown labored, a soft growl vibrating in the back of his throat, and he hissed when Cole brushed his lips against the weeping head of Nexhan's cock.

Cole grinned and lewdly licked his lips, drawing the salty taste into his mouth. He dug his nails into Nexhan's ass and opened his mouth to accept the full force of his lover. He let Nexhan guide him, his hand thrusting Cole against his thick shaft, his hips driving forward with desperate need. Cole accepted it all, swallowing him down with fervor. When Nexhan twitched inside Cole's mouth, he knew he'd brought him to the edge.

Nexhan gasped and tugged Cole away from him by his hair, urgency and frustration warring on his face. His dick bobbed inches from Cole's lips and when Cole tried to close the distance, Nexhan tugged him back.

"Give me this," Cole pleaded. Sucking cock was his thing. He loved it, needed it and he wanted to feel all that power rush down his throat as surely as the cat craves the thrill of the hunt.

His words seemed to please Nexhan and the next thing Cole knew, he was being suffocated. And oh, it was glorious! He growled hungrily against Nexhan's cock and urged Nexhan to slam against him, swallowing down all that demand.

The Rune Fang let loose some sounds that made Cole almost believe Nexhan had shifted to his cat, the growls and groans feral and fierce. Cole swallowed compulsively to fight back the gag reflex, taking all that the male had to offer until his chin met Nexhan's balls. Cole dug his nails into flesh as his lover flexed his hot ass, driving forward until Nexhan let out the deafening roar that had been building in his chest. Hot cream rushed down Cole's throat and he welcomed it, sucking harder, stroking his tongue along the underside of Nexhan's shaft.

Nexhan promptly drew away from Cole, his eye furious, his cock glistening. Cole was willing to bet the male wasn't caught off guard much, nor did he lose control often. He might be pissed that Cole had an unintended effect on him, but Nexhan was fully satisfied. Cole smirked and licked the remnants of Nexhan's orgasm off his lips. Nexhan flared his nostrils, perhaps scenting Cole's arousal then smiled wryly. There was danger in that grin, a promise that his momentarily lapse of command would be reinstated with brutality, but anticipation tumbled in Cole's stomach.

Nexhan stalked back to him, falling to his knees and diving in to take Cole's mouth. The kiss was gentle, testing, and Cole opened himself up to his lover. He shut his eyes, letting Nexhan stroke him, arouse him until he was mindless. He'd never been kissed like this. It was gentle yet thorough.

Then suddenly, something crashed into his chest, the force sending him on his back against the wild growth. He laughed as Nexhan fell upon him, splitting his legs with his wide girth. Cole fully embraced the heat of the male's skin against his own, even feeling a laugh bubble up, but his mirth was quickly hushed as Nexhan sucked Cole's nipple into his mouth. Cole relaxed, enjoying the sensation of the wet warmth against his sensitive skin. Nexhan gave his nipple a playful flick before coming up to Cole's eye level.

They locked gazes for a long moment, just staring in each other's faces. Cole was still hard and Nexhan's weight against him only increased his desire. Cole was of mind to ask what his problem was, but the tenderness in Nexhan's eyes stilled him.

"Kale is your brother. Why the animosity?" Nexhan inquired, running a finger across Cole's jaw.

Cole sighed and tried to look away, but Nexhan wouldn't let him. "I don't want to talk about it."

"Sibling rivalry?" the Rune Fang asked.

"Kale is a bastard," Cole snapped then rotated his hips in an effort to convince Nexhan to drop the subject and get to the point. His point.

"You're being childish," the male stated simply.

"Am not."

"Too."

"Not. I just want to fuck," Cole grumbled.

"I'm not moving until you tell me," Nexhan grinned playfully.

Cole growled. "Who's being childish now?"

Nexhan laughed as Cole tried to wiggle out from under him. The Rune Fang threw his weight into Cole and it was like a buffalo had sat on him. He made a sound of supreme displeasure. "Why is it so important to you?"

"Family is a precious thing, Cole. You should cherish it. You don't know how long you'll have it."

The look in the man's eyes stole Cole's bluster and he sighed, defeated.

"I don't want him to get any ideas," Cole admitted.

Nexhan lessened some of his weight and urged Cole to continue.

"That I'm..." Cole looked away. "That I like..."

After a few moments of silence, Nexhan asked, "That you're a lover of males?"

Cole nodded and before he could sigh with relief that it was out, Nexhan growled angrily and got up. Cole sat up and blinked, confused.

"Cubs these days!" he roared, pacing. "You spend too much time in the cities and get these ridiculous human notions in your heads!"

"I'm not a cub!" Cole growled back.

"No, you're not," he conceded, running an appreciative glance across Cole's body. "But sometimes you act like one."

Cole bristled. He'd thought that Nexhan would understand if he'd let him in. Nexhan had run from his family, so there must have been a reason. Cole gritted his teeth and shot to his feet.

"Fuck you! I don't need this shit!" He stalked toward the trees, tripping over vines that seemed to reach for him.

"Cole!" Nexhan called.

Nexhan caught up to him and wrapped his big arms around Cole so that he was unable to go any farther. Though he knew it was useless to struggle against the Rune Fang's superior strength, he tried anyway.

He growled. "Let me go!"

"I'm sorry," Nexhan purred, holding Cole close. "I shouldn't have said that. I didn't mean to hurt you. I just don't understand why you're running from everything—especially from your family."

He buried his face against Cole's neck and Cole thought he felt a tear.

"One moment they are here," Nexhan whispered, "and the next…gone."

Cole swallowed a lump, not sure what to do or how to handle the male's emotions, but he suddenly wanted to voice his problems. He said solemnly, "I'm such a huge disappointment to them." He could tell Nexhan wanted to refute that point, but the male remained quiet, giving Cole a chance to speak while holding him tenderly.

"They want me to mate a female who I don't, and never will, love. I haven't told them I'm gay because I don't want to disappoint them further."

Nexhan sighed against Cole's neck, his breath a warm touch. He stroked Cole's abdomen soothingly. "Cole, you do know you could take a breed-mate if you desired cubs in the future, a mate whom you choose, whether male or female?"

Huh? Cole frowned and turned in Nexhan's arms so that he could face him. Nexhan's eyes were impossibly warm and yellow, like the sun on a cold winter's day. "Um, mind saying that in English?"

Nexhan sighed distastefully then smiled ruefully. "My point, exactly. Young males don't know their history these days, nor does it seem their people's traditions. A breed-mate is a sort of union where a male and a female agree to copulate in order to produce offspring. This was common with same-sex matings and with females going into heat who wished for children and weren't yet mated."

Cole pinched his eyes. "Hold on. Let me digest that for a moment. You're saying that I don't actually have to marry her and I can mate a male, but if we ever wanted"—he swallowed, not sure if he could say it since he wasn't ready to be a father—"kids, then Bess and I could hook up?"

Nexhan chuckled. "Yes, that is right in so many words."

"Why didn't my parents ever tell me?" he asked.

"Why didn't you tell them you have a preference for males?"

Cole smacked himself in the forehead. *Wow.* How could he be so stupid? It all made sense now. He had given them no indication he preferred males, so they didn't see any reason to inform him of his options.

"You want to know what I think? Maybe they just wanted to see you happy, and you hadn't given them any reason to think that being mated to a female would make you unhappy. Did you ever give them any indication that you weren't, as you'd say, 'into' this female?"

Cole thought about that for a moment. "I guess not. I really liked spending time with her. She seemed genuinely interested in the human world like I am. She'd even wanted to tag along once, but her responsibilities as Earth-Touched wouldn't allow her that. I guess… I guess I can see how my parents might think that we were… Well, in love." Cole considered is own words for a moment. "Shit. You're right. I guess I can understand how they got the wrong idea. But, that still doesn't mean that I'm not a fuck-up."

Nexhan growled and threw Cole to the ground, holding him down with his bulk. "I'll not hear that from your mouth again."

"Fine, you won't, but just because you don't want to hear it doesn't mean it's not true," Cole grumbled.

Nexhan looked at Cole with sadness then embraced him, the male's body making Cole feel as though he were bundled in a security blanket. He didn't want anyone's pity, but he was too comfortable and Nexhan felt too good against him. Cole wrapped his arms and legs around the man, realizing just how badly he'd missed another shifter's touch.

"Everyone has a purpose, Cole. Don't think for a moment that there aren't people who love you unconditionally, regardless of your imperfections," Nexhan whispered against Cole's neck.

Cole wanted to look away, but held Nexhan close to him. Let the man argue his point, but Cole knew he was wrong. Yeah, he knew his parents loved him, but that didn't change the fact that there was something wrong with him. Playing it cool, he asked, "So, are you done lecturing me?"

Nexhan chuckled and ran his lips across Cole's neck lightly. "Why? You got something more important to do?"

Cole purred. "I can think of a few things." Then he ran his hand across the male's back and gripped his ass snugly.

Laughing, Nexhan said, "I like that suggestion." The Rune Fang didn't wait for a response, just slid down Cole's body and planted loving kisses on his abs.

Cole let his head fall back against the grass and closed his eyes, concentrating on Nexhan's ministrations. The cool air against the inferno of his arousal shocked him, but the hot breath that slid across his skin gave him chills. He relaxed, his arms flung out to his sides as he concentrated on Nexhan kissing, licking and sucking. The dew-moistened vines curled around his digits like babies' fingers and the flowers opened and leaned toward him. A soft moan escaped his lips as Nexhan grasped his cock in one big, rough palm, stroking him slowly.

"You taste like summer rain," Nexhan commented absently, lapping at Cole like a thirsty dog.

Cole smiled dumbly, blinking upside down at the blooming roses. He gasped when Nexhan took his cock into his mouth and swallowed him, a gush of flower-sweet scents filling him. The grove awakened again and Cole couldn't help feeling that they had an audience. Nexhan didn't seem to notice or care as he sped up his strokes and enjoyed the weight of Cole's balls. The male whipped Cole's legs over his shoulders and wrapped a powerful arm around his hips so that Cole was unable to move his lower body. Vines twined circled his arms so that he couldn't move them either. Something touched his hair. It was as if their twosome had become a threesome. Somewhere in the back of Cole's mind, it freaked him out, but he was too caught up in the haze of pleasure to do anything about it.

Not to mention being pinned down and unable to get away while he was pleasured was extremely erotic.

Somewhere in the distance, he heard a crow cry. For the first time in a long while, he truly felt connected with everything, like another link in the chain, helping to hold the rest together.

Cole groaned deep in his throat as his orgasm built. He wanted to dig his hands into Nexhan's petal-soft locks while the Rune Fang slurped and suckled at his cock. Somehow sensing his desire, the vines tightened their grip on him. Cole heard himself whisper something through a parched throat, but he was unsure what it was — it could have been a desperate plea or an excited bark.

A wicked wind swept down from the branches, the sound of thousands of leaves rustling carried on the breeze masking whispered words. Cole lolled his head, balled his fists and growled against the assault, the impending explosion close to the surface. He tried to rock his hips up into Nexhan's mouth, but the male's grip was too strong.

Everything spun around him—at least it felt like it. He tried to pull at the vines, but they tightened. A soft buzz raced through him, the gentle vibrations turning harsh and wild. He thought he heard birds singing, but the rustle of the leaves was too loud, the electricity coursing through his body too vivid. It all coalesced into a sudden burst of ecstasy as the orgasm exploded out of his shaft. He voiced his pleasure openly and watched the colors dance on the backs of his eyelids. Reds and greens, blues and yellows swirled in a confusing dance before him as wave after wave hit him. They came together to make new colors, scattered then repeated the process, mixing and churning until they colored the ground green, the trees brown and painted the leaves the color of autumn.

Wait? Something wasn't right. *What am I seeing?* He craned his head, trying to will his eyes open, but the vision took hold of him and the weakness from the release disabled him. He noticed the trees weren't those of oak and evergreen like the forests surrounding his village, nor those of the redwoods. Their trunks were twisted, swayed by the wicked winds and the leaves looked like pitchers made to hold sweet nectar. The foliage that covered the ground glowed with an inner fire, the flowering plants sporting exotic shapes. Above him, the sky was cloudless and deep blue, almost violet, where the subtle shape of three moons hovered—

"Cole!"

Cole flipped his eyes open, a handsome face smiling at him uneasily. "Huh?"

"Are you okay?" Nexhan chuckled.

He blinked for a few moments then grinned stupidly. "You're a great cock-sucker."

Nexhan's eyes flared for a moment at the jab then he growled, pleased, and ran his fingers through Cole's hair. "Hmm, apparently so."

Cole quickly forgot about the weird zone-out and relaxed against his lover, Nexhan's gentle fingers soothing him into a peaceful sleep.

I could stay like this forever. Sleep finally took him.

Chapter Seven

Nexhan rolled around and felt a big, dumb grin stretching across his puss. Cole lay snuggled next to him, the cougar comfortable on his stomach with his arms folded under his head, snoring softly. His hair went in many directions, mussed from their play and the skin around his neck and shoulders was blemished from Nexhan's kisses.

Nexhan sighed contentedly. It felt good to wake next to a warm body. He quickly lost his smile as a pang of guilt jabbed him. *It shouldn't be him.*

"Cole?" he whispered, running his fingers through the man's cowlicks. "Time to wake up. We have a big day ahead of us."

The cougar shifted and moaned something intelligible then went right back to sleep. Nexhan's worries fled and he chuckled in delight, sliding his arms around Cole from behind. He planted sweet kisses on top of the rough marks he'd left and stroked the shifter's midsection gently.

Cole stirred and said sleepily, "That tickles."

"I know," Nexhan teased. He'd discovered that the cougar was quite ticklish last night and had vehemently exploited the fact.

"Cut it out." Cole smiled, protecting his exposed belly.

"It's well past dawn. We have a lot to do to prepare for the coming of the full moon tonight," Nexhan reminded. "And you"—he urged Cole to face him—"need to stop running. I'm sure your brother has already arrived."

Cole made a disgusted face. "Kale is a pain in the ass."

"And trust me when I say, you'll miss that ache if he were gone," Nexhan remarked solemnly.

Cole sighed wearily then smirked. "I don't think the aches you've caused will go away anytime too soon."

Nexhan laughed and kissed his lover fiercely. Cole dug his nails into Nexhan's skin, trying to pull him closer, their bodies tangling. Nexhan's cock stiffened, but he swiftly quelled his desires. "Don't think so, cub. Your wiles will have no effect on me today. Business now—play later."

Despite the jab at his youth, Cole beamed. "That's what you think."

Nexhan grinned from ear to ear and laid a hard slap on his lover's ass. "Don't make me spank you."

The cougar growled, clearly on board with the plan, but Nexhan moved away and got up, stretching. The cool night air passed slowly, leaving the new growth laden with dewdrops and giving the grove a shimmering appearance. The fog was thick and backlit by the rising sun, making it glow. The dawn had the makings of a fine day, and Nexhan couldn't wait to get on with the business of preparing for Adam's celebration. He looked down at Cole, who remained stretched shamelessly across the grass, his magnificent body displayed enticingly, eyes hooded and a pink tongue languorously tracing his bottom lip.

Delight gripped Nexhan and he held out a hand. Cole took it and tried with all his might to pull Nexhan down.

"You big bastard." Cole laughed.

Nexhan tugged Cole to his feet then ruffled the cougar's hair. "Come. I'm sure the others are wondering where I am."

"As if it's not obvious?" Cole said distractedly, trying to unwrap his foot from a grasping vine. When the shifter finally got himself free, the vine wiggled and curled as if desperate for Cole's touch. "This shit is so weird."

The flowers opened and the plants leaned toward Cole, grasping for him in desperation.

Nexhan remarked, "They seem to like you."

Flabbergasted, Cole looked at him. "Since when do plants *like* anything? That would imply that they actually *think*."

Shrugging, Nexhan had no answer. "Come," he said, slinging an arm around the man's shoulders and planting a kiss on his head. "There is much to do."

"If they don't stop being so touchy-feely all the time, I'm going to chop them all down," he shouted, as if that would frighten the foliage. It only excited them more.

Huh. Apparently they know Cole's voice.

"I'll ask Nakoda. He's a bit of a scholar. If anything, he'll…"

"Um, I'd prefer to keep this between you and me, if possible," Cole said awkwardly.

"Okay. I'll search our records for accounts of wild growths. I'm sure I'll find something in there,"

Nexhan said as they left the grove. He swore he could hear the sad cries of simple creatures.

"How far back does your library go?" Cole asked, intrigued.

"Just before we left Shairobi. I've read accounts of preparations and the journey to the gates. Some of it is hard to read, though, as the scrolls were written in various dialects."

Cole stopped at blinked at him. "Wow. That old?"

Nexhan nodded. "It's really amazing that we've been able to preserve what we have."

The shifter bit his lip. "What do you suppose it's like—Shairobi?"

Nexhan considered the question for a moment. "I would suppose it's nothing at all like this earth. In Shairobi, things are wild, free and unchecked. At least that's what my father told me when I asked him the same question. The truth is, no one knows—or more accurately—remembers. Most of the elders are gone and what little writings we have are vague."

Cole followed Nexhan as they walked. Nexhan sensed that the cougar wanted to talk, but the blur of something small and brown caught their attention. The tiny bird sped past and flew into a tree with a soft thunk, falling lifelessly to the ground.

Startled, Cole looked at him.

Sadly, Nexhan said, "This happens sometimes, especially with the fog."

Cole moved to the tree, squatted and stared at the creature. Nexhan joined him and scooped the sparrow into his hands, its soft feathers caressing his rough palms. There was no energy flowing from the avian, no gentle thump of a heartbeat. It had been a quick death.

"It usually happens with the older ones, but this one is young," Nexhan said, his tone full of remorse as he stroked the bird with a tender thumb. "We should return it to the Mother. Hold out your hand."

"Huh?"

"I need to dig a hole," he reasoned.

"Um... Okay," Cole sputtered and cupped his hands together.

Nexhan placed the sparrow in the cradle of Cole's hands then began digging a grave. As Nexhan moved the dirt with his hands, he heard Cole sigh. He uncovered an earthworm and placed it to the side then stopped when he had a fairly deep hole. "Okay, place it—"

The bird kicked a stick-thin foot then peeped. Nexhan gasped as the gentle energy waves of life penetrated him with renewed vigor. The sparrow hopped to its feet. Its beady eyes blinked twice then with a swift hop, it took to the air and disappeared into the fog.

Nexhan looked at Cole, who didn't appear surprised at all. "I thought it was... Surely it had broken its neck?"

"Well, at least it didn't bite me," Cole mumbled then got to his feet. "Let's get back to the village."

"Cole?" Nexhan called as the male moved to walk away. Unhappy that Cole had dismissed him, he gripped the cougar's wrist and pulled him against his body.

"Hey." Cole smirked. "Play later, remember?"

Nexhan let the remark slide. He'd quickly learned that sarcasm was Cole's way of dealing with things he didn't want to address. Nexhan held the shifter's hand up and ran his fingers over the skin of Cole's palm.

Magic warmed it, but it seemed more concentrated than when *Akumai'ai* had touched Cole.

"That tickles," Cole said softly, amused. His expression, however, remained troubled.

Nexhan narrowed his eyes on him. He noticed something he'd missed before. Cole's vibrant violet eyes had tiny green flecks in them. *Or maybe they hadn't been there before.* Nexhan came closer as if he were going to kiss Cole. Instead, he asked, "This is not the first time this has happened, is it?"

Cole sighed disgustedly.

"Tell me," Nexhan ordered, his tone rich with authority.

Cole regarded him wearily for a moment then conceded. "I was nine and was walking in the woods with Kale. We stumbled upon some raccoons fighting. I wanted to help, but Kale said it was the way of life and not to interfere," Cole explained snappily, clearly upset by the memory of his older brother. "So we left, but on the way back I found one of the raccoons just lying there. It was bloody. I thought it was dead and picked it up, meaning to bury it, but it woke up and bit me. Then it ran off. Apparently it had been playing dead for shits and giggles, just waiting for some idiot to touch it." He stepped away from Nexhan and crossed his arms defiantly. "The shithead laughed at me."

Nexhan absorbed Cole's story. It was probably just a big coincidence. The raccoon had been injured, but not fatally. The bird had probably just knocked itself out, but Nexhan's instincts screamed that the creature had in fact been dead. Had he been in the city so long that his instincts were now skewered? Nexhan pulled Cole back against him and traced Cole's bottom lip with his thumb.

Growling, Cole shoved him away. "I don't need your pity!"

Completely lost at the man's outburst, Nexhan growled back. "I wasn't trying to coddle you! I'm simply trying to understand you. Why do you feel the need to run every time someone tries to get close to you?"

Cole chuckled, his eyes becoming hooded. "I've let you get *verrrry* close."

The tone had been sexual, but Nexhan wasn't going to let Cole get away. "Emotionally, you keep yourself locked behind a metal wall."

That drained Cole's bluster. He sighed and looked away, probably debating whether to lash out with foul words or run — maybe both. Nexhan stayed where he was, waiting for the cougar to make the first move, prepared to dash after him if necessary. He was surprised when Cole started talking.

"There's something wrong with me," Cole admitted, the hurt evident in his voice. Clearly it had taken a lot for the shifter to admit that.

"What do you mean?" Nexhan asked softly, not wanting to scare him into locking up again.

Cole backed up to a tree and ground his molars. "I...don't know."

"Try to explain it as best as you can," Nexhan urged.

Cole looked like he wanted to hit something again, his expression lost between frustration and anger, pain and confusion. "Sometimes, I feel as though I'm caged. Like there's something inside me wanting to get out but I have no idea what it is or how to release it. I get these weird vibrations inside, like it's trying to remind me that it's still there."

Nexhan watched Cole as he spoke, the cougar's gaze glued to the ground, but the relief of voicing his private thoughts evident in his body language. Nexhan had heard similar words spoken before many years ago. Cole was suddenly loose, relaxed. He bumped his head against the tree and looked at Nexhan in expectancy.

"Have you ever spoken to Storm?" Nexhan scratched his chin.

Cole laughed as if Nexhan had just asked why the grass was green. "He talks to nobody."

"Point taken," Nexhan laughed wearily. Damn, he needed to talk to that male, set their past straight. He had intended to do so the night of his return, but things had gotten...busy. "There are no shamans in your clan at the present."

"What does that have to do−?" Cole blinked at Nexhan with wide eyes. "What are you saying?"

"But there have been shaman in the Nicoyla line. Quite a few actually, if I remember correctly," he whispered then sighed, offering Cole a smile. "Nothing. Not yet. Come here," he commanded. When Cole didn't move, Nexhan snarled, daring the cougar to defy him. "Come here."

Cole tsked at him, pasting an expression of youthful annoyance on his fair face but ultimately obeying. Cole's cat recognized Nexhan's dominance and urged him to be good and do as he was told. Nexhan pulled the shifter close and kissed him gently and thoroughly until Cole relaxed in his arms. Nexhan looked into the cougar's beautiful violet-green eyes, such conflicting colors and said, "Give me some time. I'll help you figure this out."

Cole considered that for a moment, digging his fingers into Nexhan's back, needing the support. "You think I'm a shaman?"

"I think you're *something*, but I can't say what just yet. I didn't notice it right away, but after spending some time with you, you're energy waves are a little different," he admitted, pushing an errant lock from Cole's eyes. "It is not uncommon for our people to sit around campfires and tell stories of old—stories that seem ridiculous, stories of heroes boasting amazing abilities. All the fables are really just reinterpretation taken from our long history back to the days when we ran the forests of Shairobi. My time with the Loupen showed me this. I met one who can make people do things with his mind. Another could track you to the ends of the earth with the taste of your blood."

"Really?"

Nexhan nodded. "Who knows what we lost when we left and who knows what we held on to—perhaps things long laid dormant that all those who knew of them have passed and all those who now live have forgotten they even once existed."

Cole pursed his lips in thought then grinned. "Okay, old man."

Nexhan growled, delighted that the carefree Cole he had grown to care for had returned. "Not old enough to give your ass a thorough kicking."

"Mmm, that sounds tempting," the cougar purred.

"Very tempting," Nexhan conceded, taking his lover's lips again, tasting that peppermint spice. "But, alas. We have stuff to do."

Cole sighed and let Nexhan lead him toward the village, Nexhan's arm around his shoulders and Cole's wrapped behind Nexhan's back. It was a lover's embrace, more than a friend's or brother's sharing of comfort, and that scared Nexhan. It made the hurt and guilt he'd tried to bury bubble up to the surface. It shouldn't be Cole at his side this moment—

it should be someone else. And yet, Cole felt right against him, even if his heart cried for the touch of another.

I have to let go of him. Let go of the past. Live here, in the now. He's moved on and I have to too. It's time to look ahead, not back.

Nexhan glanced at the cougar next to him, who was busy scowling at the sound of a cawing crow. He was so handsome, his face caught between boyishness and maturity, his eyes bright and alive. His strong, muscular body against Nexhan's own appeared to be a near perfect fit. Nexhan could see himself walking among the Red Daughters with Cole next to him as they watched the first snows fall, watched as the spring grass grew and felt the warm breeze of summer against their skin as they lay naked on the ground. It was a very real possibility that held the promise of better times. Nexhan knew Cole wanted more than just physical pleasure, he could see it in the cougar's eyes, feel it in his energy. The shifter was desperate for acceptance and companionship, though he might deny it. And truthfully, so was Nexhan.

It was there if he dared to take it.

But, things weren't as simple anymore. He was clan leader. He had to think about more than just his own desires, his own needs. He was responsible for many lives.

He'd help Cole, though, as he'd promised. That was one thing he was sure of.

* * * *

"Don't run away," Nexhan ordered, his tone ripe with authority. "Or I swear, I'll chase you down and spank you and it won't be very pleasurable."

Cole grumbled at Nexhan as he avoided eye contact with his brood-brother. Kale was sitting with some Rune Fangs and the creepy eagle-shifter around a dead campfire, enjoying a cup of tea and chatting freely. The Rune Fangs seemed genuinely interested in what was going on with the cougar clan these days and Kale was suddenly the big man on campus. *That bastard.*

Cole heard Nexhan issue another stern warning behind him and Cole snapped, "I'm not running, just going to my room to get dressed!"

Of course, his little outburst succeeded in drawing his brother's attention and the male rose to his feet, cutting off Cole's escape. "Bro! I've missed you!" he said with enthusiasm, a gentle smile on his face.

Suspicious, Cole cocked an eyebrow. "Really?"

"Of course. Who else am I going to pick on?" he teased, his vibrant blue eyes twinkling like stars. Kale was six years older and he looked and acted every bit the spoiled eldest child. He had the same sandy-colored hair and light complexion as Cole, but it was his cocky, confident expression he wore religiously that separated them. Cole knew *he* had a sarcastic streak, but compared to Kale, he was a kitten.

Scowling at his brother, Cole should have known better. "Well, you can just go back. You're not needed here and I don't want you here."

"Actually, I'm the official emissary sent to offer our clan's congratulations to the new cub. Sorry, you're stuck with me for a few days." He beamed.

Cole could almost see all the nasty little pranks forming in his brother's mind. Cole sneered at his brother and made for his cabin. When he noticed Kale was following him, he snapped, "Why are you following me?"

"I'm just curious to see how you're getting along here." Kale's eyes flickered for a moment. "Did they set you up with a nice crib?"

It was best to keep quiet. Cole knew no matter what argument he might put up, all he'd succeed in doing was wasting his breath. His brother wanted to see his living quarters then nothing but the end of the earth was going to stop him. *Fine. What will it hurt?* Like there was anything more than a bed and some strewn clothes to see? Cole huffed as he made his way to his crash pad, a cabin about the size of a big closet—just enough room for a bed, a dresser and a writing desk. He sensed Kale looming behind him, the male's gaze drilling into him.

Leading his brother into his cabin, Cole spread his arms out. "There. You've seen my place."

Kale sighed with amusement and plopped his ass on Cole's makeshift bed. Cole glared at his older brother, wanting to sink his claws into his ass to get him up and out.

"I have something for you." Kale smiled buoyantly at him

"I don't want anything from you," Cole bit out, folding his arms across his chest. He should have just retreated into the forest. At least there he would have enjoyed his confrontation with Nexhan.

Cole thought he saw a look of disappointment flash over Kale's face, but Cole quickly dismissed that thought as ludicrous. Kale dug in the knapsack he had around his shoulder and handed Cole a bracelet made of polished obsidian. The stone held strong positive properties and was believed to offer spiritual protection, as well as boost the confidence of the wearer.

"From Mom. She made it—told me to give it to you."

Cole muttered a thanks and moved to lay it on a pile of clothes when he realized he was still naked. His shifter mind didn't see a problem with it, but Kale had probably noticed him and Nexhan returning together, and Cole was sure the clan had noticed they had been off together quite a bit lately... Coming back naked... Yeah, he didn't want to give his brother any ideas so he quickly yanked on a pair of old jeans and a T-shirt.

"So, what to do you do for fun out here?" Kale asked.

"Milk cows," Cole replied blankly.

"Sound like buckets of fun," Kale remarked just as blandly.

"Buckets," he agreed.

They were silent for a moment, Kale lazing on the bed, Cole leaning against the wall and the brothers staring each other down.

"Bessa misses you," Kale said, finally breaking the silence. "She wanted to come."

Dreading the topic, Cole sighed. "How is she doing?"

His brother shrugged. "You'd know if you came home."

Cole sneered and made for the door, not in the mood to put up with his brother's bullshit.

"Cole," Kale said. When Cole ignored him, Kale said solemnly, "Mom misses you. Dad too."

He stopped in his tracks and huffed. "Right. I'm sure Dad's just itchin' to start cleaning up my messes again."

For some reason beyond Cole's reasoning, his remark seemed to anger his brother.

Kale got up from the bed in a flash and confronted Cole, their noses almost touching. "Why do you say such things when you know it would hurt them?"

He didn't answer, just defiantly glared at his brother. He balled his fists, wanting to smash his knuckles into Kales face.

"It hurts me too," Kale said on an exhale, the look on his face tender

Most of Cole's bluster evaporated. Surely, this was some sort of cruel joke concocted by his brother.

"It pains me deeply to know that you don't believe me, and I know a part of that is my fault. But, you are my brother. I might be an ass sometimes — okay, *most* of the time — but I still love you."

Cole swallowed a lump. What was Kale saying? Dare he believe his brother's words? The man's body language was gentle, the energy waves radiating positive, but he'd never seen this side of Kale before. Honest. Gentle. It felt strange.

"Say something, Cole. Talk to me," Kale urged, his eyes showing desperation.

Cole blinked, opened his mouth, closed it. *Tell them,* he heard Nexhan whisper in his mind. Maybe the Rune Fang was right. He needed to talk to his family and stop pushing them away.

He had to line up the words floating in his mind, trying to make sense of the chaos. "Something is wrong with me."

Kale exhaled, apparently relieved Cole was willing to talk. "What do you mean? Is it because you're a klutz?"

Cole scowled.

His brother grinned, unable to resist the urge to tease. "Sorry. You know I'm not one to sugarcoat things. But, that's part of it, isn't it? Please, talk to me."

"It *is* part of it," Cole admitted but remained guarded.

"Who cares?" Kale huffed as if it were no big deal. "Do you think just because you have a tendency to trip over your own feet, we'd love you any less? Are you an idiot?"

Stunned, Cole blinked at his brother. Now that Kale had put his deepest fears into words, Cole felt stupid for thinking it. Reluctantly, he nodded. "I feel like such a failure. I know I disappoint Dad a lot."

A sound of disgust burst from Kale. "You *know*. Or you *think*?"

Cole didn't get a chance to respond. His brother tossed an arm around Cole's neck and pulled him in. He struggled a bit, but it felt so good to be held by his brother, to feel the flesh of his kin against his own.

"Let me tell you a story. The day before I left to journey here, Dad took me aside and asked that I try to convince you to come home. We talked for a bit and I admitted I'd been a little hard on you. I told him I wasn't intentionally trying to hurt you, but that I realized I had. That was why I demanded the clan send me as emissary, so I could apologize. Dad is angry with me, and he has a right to be. You're my baby brother. I'm supposed to protect you, look after you and I haven't."

Cole didn't know what to say. He studied the floor, a bit uncomfortable with the show of emotion from his brother, but he found himself leaning closer and closer toward him for support.

"We talked some more," Kale went on, planting a kiss on Cole's head. "He told me about the problems you were having, but how proud of you he is that you'd tried so hard to do better. He wants you to come home so that he can tell you that himself.

Nobody's perfect, Cole, not even creatures like us. Perfection belongs solely to the gods."

As he listened, Cole could barely breathe, his eyes stinging with unshed tears. He had wanted to hear those words for so long and now that he was hearing them, it felt unreal somehow. He swallowed down his emotions as Kale hugged him and Cole instantly found himself wrapping his arms around his brother, grasping at the cloth that covered the Kale's body.

Kale kissed Cole's neck. "I love you, bro. Never forget that. Even if I'm an ass, I still love you."

Helpless, as a tear coalesced in the corner of Cole's eye, he laughed and said, "You're pretty good at apologies for someone who's never given one before."

Kale chuckled. "Of course I am! I'm good at *everything*!"

Smiling, Cole pulled his brother closer. They held each other for some time, Kale apparently needing Cole's comfort just as much as he did. When Cole was sure he had a grip on his emotions, he pulled away. He was surprised to find Kale's eyes shining with moisture.

"Now. About the other stuff..." Kale urged.

Cole sighed. *Right. About that.* Did he just flat out blurt it?

"Stop acting like a human and tell our parents you like fucking dudes, and get it over with already." He said bluntly.

Cole's jaw nearly fell to the floor. "How?"

"Really?" Kale snickered. "You're really going to ask that? You think Bessa doesn't know? Females are smart, bro. Never forget that," he said, rubbing his stomach as if he'd learned it the hard way.

Bessa knew? But, Cole was sure he'd been... *Well, she is Earth-Touched after all.* Surely, she'd know a thing like that. And he hadn't exactly been affectionate with her. She must have noticed.

Kale rolled his eyes. "She didn't want to say anything for fear of scaring you, since you seemed to have such a problem making it known. She confided in me before I left."

"I...didn't..." He couldn't say anything so he bonked himself in the forehead. "I'm such an idiot."

"I agree." Kale grinned wickedly.

Laughter took over Cole and he couldn't remember the last time things had been so carefree between him and his brother.

"Now," Kale added, "any other dirty little secrets you want to reveal?"

"Hold on. I'm still recovering from shock," Cole said, surprised at the buoyancy in his voice. It felt wonderful to be so open and light with his brother. But how was he supposed to explain the 'something wrong with him' thing? Shifter or not, he felt weird telling his brother that weeds had sprung up from the ground when he'd came. "Um... It's complicated."

"Is it a guy?" Kale waggled his eyebrows. "I have to admit, these Rune Fangs are hung like—well, I'd say a horse, but that wouldn't be correct."

Cole covered his brother's mouth with his palm and groaned. The guy was shamelessly crude. Apparently, the human blood in their family ran thicker in Kale's veins. "It's not about that... Well, maybe just a little, but mostly no! Um... Nexhan says I'm something—"

"*Nexhan!* I knew it was him! Ha! Bangin' the clan leader! Score!" He made an obscene motion with his hips.

Cole was of a mind to comment that it was the other way around. Instead, he just glared. "I like the weepy, apologetic version of my brother better."

"Take pictures, bro, it's a rare occurrence. But I was never weepy," he teased.

"Uh-huh. Sure," Cole teased back.

Kale smiled. "So?"

Tell him. Trust him. Cole sighed and scratched the back of his neck. "I apparently can do...things and strange stuff happens around me."

Obviously interested, Kale cocked an eyebrow. "What kind of things? Did you know I can shoot a load seven feet? Is it anything like that?"

Exasperated, Cole laughed, not sure how to respond to that. "Um... Come with me."

"What, you want to have a contest?" Kale growled with excitement.

Cole knew his brother was being lewd on purpose. It was just who he was.

"Remind me—who's the older one here?" Cole chuckled as he led his brother out the door and toward the forest.

"Where are we going?"

"It's hard to explain, so I have to show you," Cole said, unable to believe being open with his brother was coming so easily to him. He still kind of felt a little uncomfortable with all the lovey-dovey stuff, but that was also new to him. Hell, he couldn't remember ever hugging Kale.

They walked for short while through the redwoods, Kale making absent-minded comments and asking questions about how life was with the Rune Fangs. Cole felt a little weird taking his brother to what he considered 'Nexhan and Cole's Garden of Love', but he wasn't sure how to explain what was happening with him.

To fill the silence, he asked, "Remember the raccoon? The one that bit me?"

Kale chortled. "That was so funny." He quickly sobered and after a moment, he said, "You know, I felt bad about it afterward...teasing you like that."

Stopping, Cole faced his brother. "Really?"

Kale shrugged, abashed. "What about it, anyway?"

"It was dead, you know?" he said. "But then it just...came alive again."

They started walking again.

"Yeah," Kale admitted, "I thought it was, too."

"The same thing happened earlier today. A bird flew into a tree. We were sure it had broken its neck. But it woke up and took off like nothing," Cole explained.

"*After* you touched it," Kale deduced.

"Yeah." When the scent of flowers and the earthy aroma of plant growth caught his nose, he turned to Kale and gave him a stern expression. "Swear to me right now you won't try to make a joke out of this. I'm trusting you—do you get what I'm saying?"

His brother looked him right in the eye and nodded, his voice thick with tenderness. "Yeah, I do."

Cole swallowed hard, studying his brother closely for a moment then led Kale into the grove. The flowers instantly opened and the vines awakened, reaching for him. Small insects fluttered back and forth, collecting nectar from the flowers. Cole's cheeks grew really hot as he explained to Kale what was going on. "This happened after we... Nexhan and I... Uh, hooked up. After I, um...came on the ground."

Kale chuckled, but his tone was completely serious. "Talk about planting your seed."

Chapter Eight

"Everything has been taken care of. Hihano is busy in the kitchen preparing tonight's meal and everyone has completed their share of the chores. All the necessary reagents for the ceremony have been gathered. Bruno and his mate arrived earlier as well. The bears brought some interesting gadgets with them. I haven't seen Storm yet, but I'm sure he'll return in time for the ceremony," Nakoda said and smiled with contentment. "Everyone is excited."

Nexhan nodded. He was too. It wasn't everyday a Rune Fang was born and introduced to the world. He looked around the village. It was a spark of activity, shifters zipping back and forth. "Have you seen Cole?"

"No. I assumed he was with his brother." Nakoda shrugged.

Hmph. Nexhan grumbled to himself. If the cougar had taken off, Nexhan was going to hunt him down and...he wasn't sure what, but he'd make good on his earlier threat. It wouldn't be pleasurable. The male needed to stop running from everything. In the back of his mind a little voice whispered, *hypocrite*.

"*Mi'wisa*?" Nakoda's voice was distant.

"Huh?" Nexhan blinked at his friend.

"You seem...troubled. Is there anything I can do to help?" The male spoke lightly, radiating pure energy waves of warmth.

After taking in a big, refreshing breath, Nexhan slowly let it leak out. "No. I'm fine."

Nakoda gave Nexhan a look that said he didn't quite believe him. "Well, I found some things in the library that might perk your interest. I left the tome on the desk. Look through it when you have time. Oh, look. There he is."

He followed Nakoda's gaze to the edge of the meadow. Cole's brother had an arm swung around Cole and they were taking playful jabs at each other as they strolled across the clearing. Nexhan's heart soared. He was a bit surprised, though. Cole had shown uneasiness and hostility toward his brother earlier, but they seemed to be getting along wonderfully.

Nakoda sighed with pleasure. "This is good."

Relief still whirling through him, Nexhan concurred. Maybe the cougar had talked to his brother, had finally let someone get emotionally close to him. Maybe now that Cole realized that his family would accept him no matter what, he could go home. Pain stabbed Nexhan. Did he really want Cole to go home? *Yes, if only to reconcile with his family*. He'd miss the shifter immensely, but Nexhan knew that it would be best for both Cole and himself if he returned to his clan.

Am I sure about that? Or am I just being a big baby, too wounded to deal with the possibility of a future that does not include Inari?

He growled inwardly. Now was not the time to have a private debate with himself. He turned to Nakoda to ask that he be left to speak with the cougars in private, but Nakoda was already making his way back to the center of the village. He blinked at Nakoda's strong back. Had his friend sensed his internal conflict?

Probably. Nakoda was sharp like that.

The sound of laughing on the wind caught Nexhan's attention and Nexhan smiled at the sight before him. This was right—the way it should be. Family was everything and watching Cole freely accept his brother's affections delighted Nexhan in a way he couldn't describe. There was also longing, envy for what had been taken from him all those years ago and Nexhan suddenly wondered if he were tainting Cole's moment. He made a move to give the two cougars space, but an excited voice stopped him.

"Oh, hey!" It was Kale, his expression all smiles as he guided Cole toward Nexhan. Cole growled something at his brother then looked at Nexhan and blushed. "Chill, bro. I just want to say hi. Or do you want me to be rude?"

Cole said nothing.

"Nexhan, my man!" Kale grinned.

Laughing, Nexhan tried keeping up with the cougar's strange handshake that consisted of butting fists and twisting fingers. He'd seen this greeting before, but it was something else trying to replicate it.

"How goes it?" Kale added.

"Good. Everything has been prepared for the celebration tonight. I'm extremely excited." He smiled.

"Sweet." Kale beamed. "Did anyone bring beer?"

Cole scolded his brother while Nexhan scratched his chin.

"I don't think that occurred to anyone. However, we have plenty of root beer that's in the storage shed." Shifters, by nature, did not crave the alcoholic beverages, as one wouldn't be able to get the desired effects unless he drank a lot because of the shifters' accelerated metabolisms. However, a lot of the shifters who frequented the human cities had developed a taste for the pungent brew.

"Bleh, that's kid's stuff." Kale made a face. "You can't have a party without getting drunk!"

"It's not that kind of party, doofus!" Cole chastised

Amused, Nexham laughed to himself. And he had called Cole a cub? "Well, if you ask Nakoda nicely, he might be persuaded to share some of his pipe weed."

That brightened the cougar's face. Actually, both of them. *Eh, Cole is like his brother more than he realizes.*

"I didn't know you guys smoked. I can't believe Nakoda's been holding out on me all this time," Cole complained.

Nexhan laughed. Yeah, they could be twins. "Well, the practice of smoking Caladri is usually reserved for special occasions."

Kale nudged Cole. "And tonight is a special occasion," Kale stated.

"Where are you going?" Cole scowled.

"To make friends with Nakoda." He winked then tossed Nexhan and Cole a lewd glance. "And give you two some room."

Cole glared at his brother.

When Kale was gone, Nexhan turned to Cole and smiled. "You told him."

The cougar blushed fiercely. "He already knew!"

"And here you were all this time, pouting and wallowing for nothing." Nexhan chuckled.

Cole slumped his shoulders. "Bessa told him. She knew and still… I didn't know she suspected. He's okay with it, though."

"Why wouldn't he be?" Nexhan asked.

Cole had no answer and looked at Nexhan. He had the desire to kiss the cougar right out in the open where wandering eyes could see. He didn't care so much now that someone might see. That felt good, to be honest. He vaguely wondered if he had been hiding their relationship for Cole's sake.

"I'm happy for you, Cole," Nexhan whispered.

Cole looked away, apparently uncomfortable with Nexhan's words. Before he could say anything more, a commotion went up and Nexhan sighed ruefully as he caught Hihano's aggravated energy waves. The male was running around, his gaze on the ground apparently looking for something. When he spotted Cole and Nexhan, he gasped and ran toward them.

"*Mi'wisa*! I need your help!" he shouted.

"What's the matter?" Nexhan asked, concerned.

"We are out of sorrel! I can't finish my dish without it! *Eu'tedshe* has always been served at a cub's coming out! I can't…" He huffed. "There's no one else. Everyone is busy!"

Nexhan chuckled to himself and clapped the startled male on the shoulder. "Breathe, brother. Cole and I will find some."

This seemed to calm Hihano and he took a deep breath. "Thank you, *Mi'wisa*. I just want everything to be perfect!" With that, he rushed back to the kitchen.

Cole arched an eyebrow at Nexhan. "He takes his cooking very seriously."

"Indeed," Nexhan replied, a wicked smirked on his lips. "Shall we?"

Cole started to grumble about having to scour the vastness of the forest for some silly herb, but the look in Nexhan's eyes stilled him. A slow smile spread across his face. "Well, it's for an important reason. Let's go."

Laughing heartily, Nexhan pulled Cole close to him, ruffling his hair as they walked toward the trees. Cole smiled shyly and slung his arm around Nexhan's back.

"So," Nexhan began, "tell me about your brother. He seems a lot like you."

Cole made a disgusted face. "He's an asshole. He bugs the shit out of me and most days I want to ram my knuckles in his face." He snarled then blew out a breath and added, "But, I love him."

"Siblings are often like that." Nexhan chuckled softly. "I'm glad that you two worked out your problems."

"Do you have any siblings?" Cole asked, interested. "I mean... Did. Shit, sorry."

"It's okay, I know what you meant." Nexhan drew him even closer as they passed the young redwoods. "I had an older sister, but she died a long time ago."

"What was she like?" Cole looked at him with bright eyes.

He let go of Cole and pressed his back against the bark of a spruce as he let the memories bubble up. A faint smile found its way to his lips. He could almost see her face as she looked at him and stuck her tongue out in jest. "She was beautiful. She was my twin and she had a fierceness to match my own. She was born before me and therefore was next in line for clan leader. She died in what is now known as Alaska, assisting the bear-shifters in ridding the lands of rogue Lycans. We also lost her mate that day as well... Nakoda's brother."

Cole came up to Nexhan and threw his arms around Nexhan's waist, planting a soft kiss on his lips. "I'm sorry."

Nodding, Nexhan tried to hold back his tears. "The worst thing is... We were never able to recover their bodies."

"Shit," Cole muttered, tugging Nexhan into him. Cole said against his neck. "Suddenly, my problems don't seem so important."

Nexhan dug his fingers into the cougar's hair, jerking him a bit roughly and peered into deep violet eyes. There seemed to be more flecks of green intersecting the vivid purple now. "Don't downplay your pain, Cole."

He sighed seemingly in disagreement, but kissed Nexhan on the lips. "Sorry. It's just... I don't know. Maybe you were right. I was acting like a cub."

"We all deal with our problems in our own ways," Nexhan stated, almost voicing his admission of abandoning the clan for his vengeance. "Let's not talk about such things now. Today is a good day. Tonight we will celebrate Adam and our lives with our friends."

Cole beamed at him and Nexhan's heart kicked. It meant so much to Nexhan to see Cole happy. He smiled back and kissed the cougar deeply, thoroughly, until Cole moaned against his lips. Nexhan scooped him up, holding him close, afraid to let him go. Goddess, he needed this more than he realized—he touch, the warmth, the support.

Cole chuckled against Nexhan's lips as he ran sly his fingers down Nexhan's abs. The shifter found the hem of Nexhan's jeans and quickly undid them, pulling his cock out. Cole gave him a wicked look that set Nexhan's blood afire then Cole dropped to his knees. Nexhan threw his head back against the rough bark and groaned as Cole buried his face in Nexhan's crotch. The cougar's wicked tongue skimmed over his balls and he planted soft kisses on Nexhan's shaft, teasing his crown mercilessly. Nexhan closed his eyelids and concentrated on the sensations.

Cole slinked his fingers up Nexhan's abs, his chest then pinched his erect nipples. Nexhan let loose a feral growl as Cole took him into his mouth all the way to the base. He couldn't help but to arch his back against the tree in ecstasy. He wanted to throttle the cougar for shattering his composure, but the pleasure took hold of him and weakened his will. Cole brought him to release quickly, the little sounds Cole made exciting Nexhan further.

It was a long minute before Nexhan was able to catch his breath. When he opened his eyes, Cole was grinning slyly at him. "You're not so tough, big boy. I know your weakness."

Big boy. Nexhan knitted his brows, unable to answer.

"Nex? What's wrong?" Cole asked.

Nexhan ran his fingers through his hair. "Nothing. Let's get Hihano his sorrel before he explodes."

* * * *

"You must! You are a shaman!" Nakoda reasoned, his voice thick with sadness and anger.

Nexhan and Cole entered the cabin, interrupting an apparent debate. Nakoda's stance was agitated, while Storm lazed in a chair, playing with a butter knife.

"What's going on?" Nexhan inquired.

"*Mi'wisa*! Please, you must reason with him!" Nakoda glared at Storm, who seemed bored with the entire thing.

"What is the matter?" Nexhan asked, feeling out the waves of tension between the two.

"He refuses to do the ceremony! It is his duty as shaman—"

"*Right,*" Storm corrected, his cool gray gaze shooting to Nakoda. "Implying that it's my choice if I want to bother or not."

"*Bother!* How can you say that? It's a *bother* to welcome the cub?" Nakoda snapped.

"Calm, Nakoda," Nexhan soothed, holding his brother back. He could feel the rage coursing under the man's skin, threatening to erupt. He ran a gentle hand over Nakoda's arm until the male relaxed. Nexhan turned to Storm. "Is this true? You'll not preform the ceremony?"

Storm sighed then got to his feet, his leather garb creaking. "No."

Now it was Nexhan's turn to feel disappointed. "Why?"

Storm bunched his considerable shoulders in a shrug. "I don't feel much in a celebrating mood."

"This isn't about you!" Nakoda shouted from behind Nexhan, his voice hoarse.

Nexhan sent gentle waves to his friend, trying to ease him. He then said to Storm, "Will you not do this for Adam? For Caroline? Not even for Mewah?"

Storm's eyes flared for just a second as if his very body coursed with lightning. "No, sorry."

Nexhan and Nakoda watched him make for the exit, their mouths agape in astonishment. Cole's attention bounced back and forth between them as he waited for the action. Nexhan heard Nakoda mutter a shocked "But" and he echoed the thought. Anger suddenly rose in Nexhan. He balled his fists and marched out the door to confront the male.

"Storm!" He growled.

The male strolled toward the forest as if nothing was wrong in the world.

"Stop!"

Storm turned to regard Nexhan, his expression weary, his eyes dark.

"Why are you doing this?" Nexhan demanded. "Does the clan mean so little to you? This is your family!"

Storm let go of a breath and studied the ground. "I could ask the same thing, *Mi'wisa*."

Nexhan's first instinct was to throttle the man, but he quickly snapped himself back. Hurt quickly followed. Storm was right. He should be asking himself the same thing. He had abandoned his family for his own selfish needs. *I'm a hypocrite.* How could he expect anything more from Storm when we had been unwilling to give what he himself was asking? Is that the mark of a leader? He suddenly felt like crap.

Storm sighed and looked at Nexhan with pain-filled eyes. "Forgive me. I should not have said that."

Nexhan couldn't speak. His insides twisted and he was afraid that if he opened his mouth, sobs would spill out. He watched blankly as Storm turned around on his heels and headed toward the trees, the leather of his coat swaying.

"Please understand," Storm muttered, stopping and looking to the side so that Nexhan could see his profile. "It's not that I think so little of the clan. It's just that I'm not...*worthy* of such an honor."

Nexhan watched for a long while until the form of black leather and silver hair disappeared into the trees. Still, he couldn't wrap his mind around what had just happened. A part of him wanted to chase down the male and set everything right. The other part was too much of a coward to confront their past.

'It's just that I'm not…worthy of such an honor.' But he was wrong! What had happened all those years ago was not Storm's fault. Why couldn't he see that?

And am I worthy to be clan leader? What did I do when things got thick? At least Storm has the ability to recognize failure.

"Nexhan?" Cole's voice was like a cool balm. The cougar came up to his side, his interest piqued. "Guess we're a shammy short, huh?"

"We'll figure something out," Nexhan said, looking at the male. As Cole smiled at him, his bright violet held so much promise that Nexhan thought he'd suffocate from the feeling.

"Good. Because Nakoda is about to have a meltdown," Cole said, his voice laced with amusement.

Nexhan muttered a curse to himself and rushed back into the cabin. Nakoda paced back and forth, pulling at his hair. When Nakoda saw him, he rushed to Nexhan, panic etched on his face.

"Tell me you knocked some sense into him! Tell me he's changed his mind!" He begged.

Nexhan didn't respond, just looked wearily at his brother.

Nakoda barked a curse. "What are we to do? A shaman has always performed the ceremony. We've always had a shaman!"

Cole spoke up. "We have no shammys in our clan. Our eldest Earth-Touched usually perform the ceremonies."

Nakoda regarded Cole tenderly, thankful for the sincerity. He said solemnly, "We have no Earth-Touched."

"A problem has arisen? Donoma asked, coming in. Everyone turned to regard him. "I felt the tension."

Nakoda sighed. "Storm has refused to perform the ceremony."

As Donoma took a moment to digest the news, his expression remained stoic. "I sense great turmoil in that one."

No one had to say anything to that. Donoma knew the whole story and it was just his way of stating the obvious gently.

"Why don't you do it?" Cole asked, looking at Nexhan.

Fear gripped him. If Storm considered himself unworthy, then Nexhan was ten times as worse. "I... I don't think that would be a good idea."

"It's not a *bad* idea," Nakoda corrected. "You are clan leader. It makes sense."

"Um..."

"I could do it," Donoma said, sensing Nexhan's hesitation. "Provided you don't mind someone outside of the clan preforming the rites. In fact, I would be quite honored."

Everyone just stared at the hawk, but Nexhan secretly nursed his relief.

"I know the ceremony well." Donoma smiled. "Have you forgotten who offered you at your welcoming?"

Amused, Cole looked at Nexhan then said to Donoma, "Wow, you're that old?"

"Cole," Nexhan admonished.

"I am so often reminded of my age nowadays" — Donoma chuckled softly — "that it no longer bothers me when the cubs think it's a defect. In my days, age was linear with wisdom and power."

Nexhan secretly wondered how Cole would react if he knew Donoma's other names. The elder hawk had once been worshiped as the Egyptian God Horus, though most of the elders tended to keep their old names secret and Nexhan wasn't about to betray his friend.

Cole crossed his arms over his chest and said sternly. "I'm not a cub."

"No offense, Guardian." Donoma grinned wider. "So, what say you, Gatekeeper?"

Nexhan smiled at his old friend, not just out of relief but love. He looked at Nakoda, who seemed delighted with the idea. "We would be honored to have you perform the ceremony, Lord of Air."

With that settled, Nexhan plopped in the clan leader's chair at the head of the giant dining table and watched as Nakoda retired and Donoma went to prepare for his place in the ceremony. Nexhan pinched the bridge of his nose, frustrated with Storm and himself. They needed to talk, but it seemed the time was never right to do so. Did Storm really believe he didn't belong? How wrong he was! They'd both made mistakes and it was time to correct them.

A gentle hand stroked his hair. It was Cole. Nexhan reached out until he made contact with the cougar and pulled him close, so that the male was sitting across his lap.

"Hey. This is pretty comfortable," Cole teased.

Nexhan smiled wickedly. "I still owe you for earlier."

Something flickered in the cougar's eyes. "You don't owe me anything."

Nexhan had no answer for that, so he planted a sweet kiss on Cole's lips.

"*Mi'wisa!*"

Cole grumbled something, getting up from Nexhan's lap as Mewah burst in the door.

A fool's grin seemed permanently etched on his face, his eyes wide with excitement as he beamed at Nexhan. "There you are! I've been looking everywhere for you!"

Nexhan laughed as he met his brother halfway. They embraced sharing backslaps. "Are you dizzy yet?"

"And loving it!" He smiled, his expression reflecting a happy dotting father. "I wanted to ask you something. Caroline and I have talked about it and we've decided. We want you to present Adam."

Although floored, a part of Nexhan was thrilled, the other aghast. He heard Storm's voice call him unworthy. "Ah…me?"

"We would be honored!" Mewah beamed brightly. "Who better than our clan leader to welcome the clan's newest member?"

Nexhan glanced at Cole, who simply shrugged, though he wasn't sure why he was seeking the cougar's approval. Nexhan bit his lip and returned his attention to his brother. How could he possibly refuse without hurting anyone's feelings? "*It's not about you,*" he heard Nakoda whisper. "Mewah, clan brother, I would be honored."

Nexhan thought Mewah's joy couldn't get any bigger, but intense waves of pleasure penetrated him as Mewah hugged him tightly, whispering praises and gratitude. Nexhan was truly happy for his friend and he quickly tossed the feeling of unworthiness away. This wasn't about him. This was about the cub and the clan, and if Mewah and his mate wanted Adam to be presented by Nexhan, then that was what was going to happen.

Mewah held him at arm's length and gave him a final, hard pat on the shoulder. "*Mi'wisa*, I'd better get back. Still lots to do."

Nexhan nodded and watched as the male rushed out the door. Cole leaned in and ran an appreciative eye up and down Nexhan's body. "We better get you ready for the big show."

Chapter Nine

"You look hot," Cole remarked as he ran his gaze up and down Nexhan's body.

A pair of simple Totoa hide pants made up the bulk of his ceremonial dress, but that was where the simplicity ended. Runes decorated his body in blue ink, as well as symbols of wild animals, namely big cats. Cole had had the pleasure of painting them on and he had purposely taken his time. Beads of polished stone and precious jewels lined Nexhan's arms and neck. With his hair pulled back into a loose ponytail and tied with a rope of wild ivy, he looked feral, as if he were dressing for battle rather than a ceremony.

At the praise, he let a smile forced its way onto his face. "Glad you approve."

Cole grinned and pushed back an errant lock from Nexhan's cheek but before he could move away, the vine of ivy uncurled from Nexhan's hair and tangled itself around Cole's wrist, slinking around like a snake. They both stood still, shocked by the display. Then as quickly as it had it happened, the vine slithered away from Cole and wrapped around Nexhan's head to give him a crown of ivy.

"Okay," Nexhan said weakly. "That was a bit weird."

"A bit," Cole agreed, watching as the ivy seemingly went back to sleep on top of his lover's head.

"Well," Nexhan said, touching his crown gently, "*You* don't look so bad yourself."

Cole ran his gaze down his body and smiled. A pair of designer jeans framed his legs, but that was it. Nexhan had runed his body, painted elegant symbols across his pecs. He was dressed down compared to the Rune Fang, but he had put on the obsidian bracelet his mom had made. He had never been one for ceremonies, but he was surprised to find himself looking forward to Adam's.

"Do you think I overdid it a bit?" Nexhan asked, fingering a necklace made from the molars of all sorts of different animals.

"*Over*did it?" Cole grinned as he surveyed the man. Those pants did little to hide Nexhan's potency.

"I'm serious." Nexhan hedged "This is important. I want it to be...*right*."

"Chill. You look fine," Cole soothed. "Are you nervous? You look nervous."

"I am," he conceded. "I've never presented a cub before."

Cole shrugged. "It's not like you have to do much. Just carry the kid down the aisle and dump him in Donoma's arms."

Nexhan gave him a worried expression.

"Chill. You won't drop the kid. You're not going to trip and fall with him in your arms. That's my job," Cole teased. It actually felt good being able to say that and he was a bit surprised that admitting his clumsiness to the man didn't bother him so much anymore.

Nexhan looked at Cole tenderly. "I don't... Shit."

"Don't what?" Cole cocked a brow, intrigued. For some reason the Rune Fang seemed troubled by his task.

Nexhan sighed and studied the floor for a few moments. Scratching the back of his neck, he asked, "You know what Storm told me? About why he wouldn't do the ceremony? He said it was because he wasn't worthy. And shit... I can relate."

Was he fucking serious? Cole blinked blankly at the male. He, Nexhan, clan leader of the Rune Fangs, the biggest, baddest cats around, *unworthy*? Cole almost laughed. "You're kidding right? You're perfect for the job! You are clan leader and you are strong and healthy—"

"Brawn of body doesn't determine one's worth, Cole," Nexhan said simply. "Nor does being clumsy make one unworthy."

Cole eyed the male wearily. "Point taken." Why was Nexhan so troubled with this? Why did he feel unworthy in the first place? Cole wanted to do something, say something to make him feel better, but he sucked at the comforting part. Maybe if he understood *why* Nexhan felt the way he did, he could help. Biting his lip, he asked, "You want to tell me why you feel unworthy?"

"No, not really," Nexhan said.

A chill and a bit of aggravation shot up Cole's spine. "Then why even bother mentioning it?"

Nexhan looked at him, appearing more lost than Cole felt at the moment. Cole couldn't help but to feel disappointed. He has trusted Nexhan with his secrets and yet the guy wasn't willing to do the same. Cole muttered a curse and said, "Look, if you don't want to talk about it, fine. But there are many people counting on you, especially that little bundle of fluff who could care less about all this unworthy crap. Now quit being a bitch and get your ass out there."

Nexhan's gaze went hot and Cole fully expected to be throttled. One didn't talk to an alpha male like that, especially a Rune Fang that could bite a person in half. Cole huffed and folded his hands over his chest in defiance.

Aghast, Nexhan said, "You amaze me."

"Yeah, I'm just a bowl full of Froot Loops," Cole quipped, ignoring the fluttery feeling inside that the comment gave him. He heard Nexhan chuckle softly. Cole rolled his eyes and took Nexhan's hand in his. "Come on, you big lug. You'll be fine."

Nexhan's snicker turned into a full-fledged laugh as Cole used all his strength to pull Nexhan with him. The cat dropped all resistance and Cole felt the waves of positive energy hit him. Nexhan was pleased with him.

The night was already beginning. The actual ceremony wouldn't take place until about one in the morning, when the full moon was at its apex, but everyone was getting their party hats on. All species of Shifters packed the dining cabin and a one male nursed a bonfire to life near the big redwood in the middle of the village. Laughter floated on the air and Cole couldn't help but absorb the happy feelings. All the positive emotions permeated the air, along with the smells of food. He looked back at Nexhan who smiled at him, his mood much lighter.

Nakoda spotted them and shifted his course, crashing his body into Nexhan. The male was just a bundle of joy. "I'm so excited, *Mi'wisa!*"

Laughing, Nexhan hugged his friend close. "Me too."

Cole didn't miss the uncertainty in the Nexhan's voice. His spirits suddenly dampened. Why didn't Nexhan tell him why he felt unworthy? Didn't he trust him? Anger bubbled up in Cole's throat and he almost voiced his opinion right there, but he reminded himself now was not the time. Tonight wasn't about him or Nexhan, but Adam. He'd wait until later to confront the male.

But for now, it was party time. He grinned as he spotted Kale lighting up what appeared to be smoking weed.

* * * *

Nexhan sighed as Adam fussed in his mother's arms. It wasn't quite time yet, but everyone was gathering around *Weynka Le Gai*. Cole had practically disappeared the entire evening. No, that wasn't right. The male had been present, laughing with his brother and mingling with Nakoda and the bear-shifters. But he had been...distant to Nexhan.

I shouldn't be surprised. I practically shot him down. Yeah, Nexhan had been on the verge of blurting his whole life story, but something had held him back. Fear? Maybe. Shame? Probably. He sensed that he had somehow inadvertently hurt Cole, and he needed to correct it as soon as possible. He searched the crowd but was not able to locate Cole, and the desire to track him down nipped at Nexhan.

Nexhan gazed absently at the fat moon. It hung there like a beacon of hope against the cloudless sky, a declaration against the evil that would quest to see them destroyed. He could feel the joy and pride from his brothers as well as the other shifters that had come to bear witness to this night. But Nexhan couldn't shake the negative feelings curling inside him. He wanted to run into the woods and hide behind the giant trees. *Coward.*

"*Mi'wisa?*" Mewah broke in.

"Huh?" Nexhan blinked at his friend, not realizing the male had come up to him.

"Everything is ready." He beamed then glanced to Caroline, stunning in a simple dress of Totoa hide and a crown of flowers in her hair. Adam had finally simmered down and was burbling happily in her arms.

Donoma and his mate, as well as his brother, Kawiinok, were waiting at the base of *Weynka Le Gai*. They were dressed in their best ceremonial garbs, especially Donoma, with a wreath of lilies around his shoulders and a headdress of colorful feathers. Strings of vines and flowers decorated the area surrounding the sequoia's massive base and someone had painted the tree bark with blue ink that glowed in moonlight. Torches had been thrust into the ground and shifters stood on both sides, creating a path up to Donoma.

"Ready, babe?" Mewah asked his mate.

She smiled at him then kissed Adam's head. Nexhan carefully accepted the babe, snuggling him in his arms. Adam cooed and beat his pudgy fists in the air. Seeing that the cub was content where he was, Caroline sighed with relief. Mewah beamed at Nexhan then led Caroline down the path to stand next to the hawks.

Nexhan took a deep breath to steady himself. He looked down his body to where Adam was watching him with those striking eyes. *He doesn't care what I've done or what I think of myself. He trusts me. All he knows is that I'll be there to protect him.*

"I will be," Nexhan whispered.

Adam smiled and Nexhan ran the pad of his thumb across the babe's forehead. Feeling resolve, he erected his posture and took a deep breath. Pride rushed at him, not because he had been chosen to present the babe, but because Adam was a part of their family. He would do anything to keep the cub safe and happy. He'd protect him to the very death. Adam began to fuss suddenly. Nexhan tried to shush him gently, but that only succeeded in making Adam wail. Talon stepped forward and dangled a giant lollipop in front of the babe, making smacking sounds with his lips.

"I think that's a little big for him." Nakoda chuckled.

The eagle frowned at the candy, shrugged, then licked it. Adam screamed.

"What's the matter now, bubble nose?" Cole teased as he came up beside Nexhan.

Adam instantly quieted and, when the cougar tickled the babe's stomach, Adam broke out in laughter. Nexhan couldn't help but to smile at the way the male had with the cub that not even his mother was capable of doing.

The moon slid into its apex and the runes painted on the redwood glowed. The soft murmurs of the crowd turned into silence. It was time.

Nexhan saw Donoma motion to him then began to speak, recounting the old days in Shairobi when the Mother Goddess would bless the cubs herself. He went into length for Caroline's benefit and emphasized that the entire clan raised a cub. Nexhan wondered vaguely how she was accepting everything. She seemed genuinely happy, but she was human and it was not easy changing one's habits and beliefs.

"Who presents this child to our Mother?" Donoma asked enthusiastically.

That was Nexhan's cue. He sucked in some air and smiled at the babe, who still cooed at Cole. Cole retreated and Nexhan took his first step forward. Immediately Adam began to cry. Nexhan rocked him softly but the cub was displeased, throwing his fists in the air. Nexhan was relieved when Cole snapped next to his side and made funny faces. Slowly, Adam calmed and the first hints of a smile pulled at the corners of his mouth as he watched Cole.

"Walk with me," Nexhan whispered to Cole.

Cole didn't respond but followed when Nexhan began moving down the aisle. He sensed the happiness radiating from his brothers as he passed them and Mewah's smile was blinding as they reached the tree. Cole stayed next to him, his presence somehow comforting the child.

Nexhan cleared his throat and spoke loudly. "I present Adam Miller-Nodamasha, son of Caroline Miller and Mewah Nodamasha."

Donoma smiled tenderly at the babe. "The birth of a cub is a wondrous thing. This child is proof that our Mother still walks among us."

There was a soft clatter of agreement. Many shifters believed that the Mother Goddess had abandoned them, but with the fruitful union of a shifter and human, it was clear that was not the case. Still, Nexhan knew there would be a few disbelievers and he was a bit surprised to see that Cole was one of them. The cougar rolled his eyes, a slight gesture barely noticed.

Donoma glanced at the moon then turned to his mate, who held a wooden bowl. The hawk dipped his fingers into the sap then said some words in the old language. He gently spread the sap across the babe's forehead and Adam made a sound of delight.

"The blood of the Mother," Donoma translated for Caroline's benefit. "Will the parents step forward?"

Mewah led Caroline to stand in front of Donoma while Nexhan handed the babe off to Donoma. He and Cole scooted to the side.

Raising Adam up, Donoma spoke loudly, his words laced with good cheer. "Mother Goddess, I bid you see this child and smile upon him, so that he may live the life you wish for all your children. Let him know good health and always be loved. Let him grow surrounded by the warmth of his family and the protection of his clan. Let him walk steadily the path you have envisioned and in the long road of time, find his mate so that the circle of life may be renewed. Mother, I present to you, Adam Miller-Nodamasha of the Rune Fang!"

Everyone shouted with glee as Donoma made his proclamation and passed the child to his father. Mewah held his cub up for everyone to see and Nexhan sensed the pure joy running through him. The cub would grow strong and healthy, surrounded by love and then perhaps one day have children of his own. The possibilities were endless. With Adam's happy burble, the Rune Fangs were no longer doomed to a destiny of death. There was life and hope... *And I could have this.*

That thought sobered his cheerful mood. Never in his one hundred years after he'd lost his breed-mate had he considered it.

The bonfire wooshed as someone threw a fresh log onto it. They all passed Adam around from shifter to shifter and the proud parents were the victims of very enthusiastic well wishes. Someone played a windpipe in the background and slowly, people began to settle around the fire. Nexhan accepted the friendly pats stoically. He couldn't help but to smile as he watched his family bustle with happiness. Mewah took his seat against one of *Weynka Le Gai*'s giant roots. Caroline snuggled in front of him, with Adam cuddled in her arms. The ceremony had always been short and to the point, but it was a tradition afterward to recount the story of their creation.

Nexhan took his seat next to Donoma. He looked around for Cole and spotted him lounging with Kale on a log, smoking pipe weed. A pang of longing to have the male in his arms as they listened to the elder hawk's stories jabbed him in the heart. Cole caught Nexhan's gaze and immediately looked away, as if it meant nothing.

Nexhan swallowed his need and waited for Donoma to begin.

* * * *

Cole yawned as he watched Kale make his way to his cabin. Everyone was winding down for the night. Adam and his parents were already nestled in their cabin. Some shifters still lingered by the dying fire, chatting softly and drinking tea. Sleep coaxed him to follow, but his body hummed with energy. He didn't want to go to bed, but he didn't know what to do with himself, either. The ceremony had gone smoothly, and though he had been bored with the elder hawk's lengthy story, Cole had enjoyed himself.

Although, the way that weirdo eagle had been staring at him creeped him out... *Hey, maybe Talon is a lover of males too?* That thought intrigued him, but that was unlikely. The raptor's gaze had been searching, penetrating, as if he were purposely trying to intimidate Cole. *Whatever.* Cole had realized there was something loose in the eagle's head.

The urge to go to Nexhan was powerful, but he was angry with the man. He hadn't realized it before, but he was hurt that Nexhan didn't trust him enough to share his feelings. It really shouldn't bother him so much, but it did and that was a completely different issue—one he wasn't willing to explore at the moment. He should just go hang with Kale, finish off the pipe weed they'd pilfered from Nakoda's cabin and sleep the rest of the week in a stupor.

"Hey," Nexhan said, coming out from behind a cabin as if he'd been waiting there.

Cole blinked at him. "Hey."

"Got a minute?" Before Cole could brush him off, he added, "I want to show you something."

Not interested, Cole was tempted to say. Instead, he shrugged and let Nexhan lead him back toward the big tree. He watched blankly as Nexhan searched the ground for something. He found it and tugged on a root of the redwood. Cole watch astonished as the root came free, Nexhan yanking it with apparent ease.

At Cole's confused look, Nexhan smiled. "Here."

He handed Cole the root and that's when Cole realized it wasn't a root at all but a rope. Now that he held it in his palms, he realized that it had been disguised by magic. It was a neat thing to see, as the cougar clan didn't possess this kind of magic. Come to think of it, he didn't think any other shifters commanded such magic anymore, except maybe the hawks.

"Tricky. You know, you guys could make a killing with a magic show in Vegas," Cole remarked absently.

Nexhan stared at Cole, amused, then took the rope back. He tugged hard, his shoulders bunching as he put a lot of effort into it. Something creaked and the ground moved. A flat metal plate slid to the side, revealing a stairway that led deep underground.

"Whoa, I would have never known this was here." Cole gaped.

"It is where we store our most valuable possessions," Nexhan explained.

Cole raised his eyebrows rose at that. "And now I know where it is."

"I trust you, Cole," Nexhan said softly.

Hmph, right. Cole huffed, folding his arms over his chest. He didn't say anything.

Nexhan craned his head toward the stairs. "Come."

Cole followed the Rune Fang down the stairs. Nexhan was so tall, he had to crouch down, else he'd bump his head. When they reached the bottom, the passage expanded to allow them to pass through comfortably. Cole's night vision kicked in, surprising him with what he saw. Thick roots roofed the passage like a tangle of snakes but chiseled stone composed the floor and walls. The way was clear of debris and the air should have been musty, but it wasn't. In fact, it was fresh and flowery.

He looked at Nexhan. "More magic?"

Nexhan nodded. "Our archives were built around *Weynka Le Gai* and the natural magic that flows through her protects these halls and keeps its secrets safe."

Cole said nothing, just ran his fingers across the rough-cut stone. Warm, it hummed humming with magic, and something connected with him. It was as if the magic was made of tiny fibers and sticky like spider webs so that it clung to him. He tried to pull his hand back, but it wouldn't let go and the harder he tried, the tighter the magic held on. Cole looked to Nexhan for help, but he was already making his way down the passage.

"Wait!" Cole called out. "Help! It won't let go."

Nexhan rushed back to Cole. "Sorry. I should have told you. The magic is a little wild down here."

"Wild?" Cole said aghast. "It won't fucking let go."

"Easy," Nexhan soothed, placing a hand on Cole's shoulder. "We don't come down here very often. It must be reacting to our presence."

"I'm the one that's stuck! I can't get my hand loose." He hissed more frustrated than startled now.

"Relax. Just give it a moment," Nexhan purred in his ear.

Cole tried to calm himself, but the magic was thumping through him like techno music, getting his blood pumping and his body vibrating. Nexhan came up against his back and Cole took a deep breath. He leaned against the male for support and decided to let the magic flow through him rather than fight it. Colors burst across the back of his eyelids and a dazzling display of vividness and warmth surrounded him.

Nexhan made a sound of discomfort. "That's strong."

"You can feel it?" Cole asked, as he took steady breaths.

"You're like a conductor. It's using you as a medium," he said, his voice soft. He'd relaxed, his body warm and enveloping against Cole's. "This is why Storm doesn't like coming down here. The magic has a tendency to reach for those gifted by the Mother. I've felt the magic through him before, but never this *powerful*."

Cole swallowed hard. He was doing his best to remain calm, but the vibrations under his skin were starting to become painful. He swore the magic zapped through him relentlessly.

The discomfort subsided abruptly and a soothing peace filled him. It was like liquid warmth all around him and inside him, filling his soul with comforting heat. He moaned and let his head fall back against the sturdy chest behind him. His eyelids grew heavy and his body loosened. It was a feeling akin to lazing on the spring grass on a hot summer's day with no desire to do anything. Slowly, he felt his hand being peeled away from the wall, the magic that had bound him letting go.

"Shit," Nexhan muttered.

"Yeah," Cole sighed dreamily.

He heard Nexhan chuckle softly before grinding his hips against Cole's back. He had a hard-on. Cole looked down his body and snickered at his own erection. "What just happened?"

"Magic," Nexhan said simply. It explained everything—and nothing.

Cole found his balance, swayed then righted himself. He turned to regard Nexhan, who was smiling at him tenderly. Cole glanced at his palm. It was warm, sweaty, as if he'd been holding on to something hot for a while. "You said *Akumai'ai* recognized me. It burned me too, just like this."

Nexhan's lips went tight and he nodded. "The magic has recognized you."

"What. Exactly. Does. That. Mean?" he bit out.

"Ah…" Nexhan scratched his chin. "I'm not sure how to explain it, seeing as it's never touched me personally. Not the way it does with you."

"Does magic recognize Storm?" Cole asked.

"Yes," he answered. "But never to this degree. At least, I don't think so."

"You're not sure?"

Nexhan sighed wearily. "We don't talk much anymore."

Cole bit his lip, wanting to ask why that was. Instead, he sighed. "Okay, so you said it has a habit for recognizing the gifted. Does that mean I'm...*something*?"

Nexhan stepped forward and pulled Cole to him by his neck. He opened his mouth to say something, but the only thing that came out was a muttered moan as the Rune Fang kissed him hungrily. He could do nothing but respond as their tongues tangled feverishly. He wanted to push Nexhan away. He was still mad at the male, but the kiss was too enticing. His already aroused state welcomed the stimulation openly.

Nexhan broke away and smirked. "You *are* something. That is one thing I'm sure of, Cole. I said I'd help you figure this out and I intend to keep that promise."

Cole blinked at him for a moment then shrugged. "Yeah, sure."

His lover made a guttural sound then gripped Cole's ass so tightly, he was sure he was going to bruise. "Don't give me that attitude. When I say I'm going to do something, I do it. Do you understand?"

"Yeah, I got it," Cole grumbled, unable to contend with Nexhan's dominance.

Nexhan softened then planted a chaste kiss on Cole's lips. "Good. Then follow me."

Cole let the Rune Fang take the lead and followed. He believed Nexhan. He had no reason not to. He just wished the man would trust him with his pain.

"Oh, and you might not want to touch anything else," Nexhan suggested.

"Good idea." Cole sneered at the roots above him.

He remained quiet as he followed Nexhan. The passageway angled to the side and it was clear as they passed down several short flights of stairs that they spiraled deeper into the earth.

"We are going pretty far down."

"The archives were built around the tree's root system," Nexhan explained. "That is part of the reason why the magic is so strong here."

Nexhan stopped in front of a door and whispered some ancient words. The lock clanked and the door slowly creaked opened. Cole watched astonished as invisible waves of magic pulsed gently around him. A soft vibration buzzed through his body.

"It's searching you, reading your energy for any hints of ill intent," Nexhan said. "It's our security system. Should anything vile trying to enter, the magic will suck them dry. It's how we..."

Cole waited, but Nexhan just stood there, apparently frozen by memories he seemed uninterested in sharing. He felt the male's sudden sadness and was tempted to hug him close, but when Nexhan brushed him off, Cole huffed to himself.

"Anyway, suffice to say, they wouldn't live to tell the tale," he said then led Cole into the room. He whispered some more words and suddenly the room flared to life.

Cole watched as the sconces and braziers burst with green flames, illuminating the room in a bath of soft light. The immense magic around them seemed suffocating, and he winced.

"There are a lot of magic-imbued things here. Sometimes it can feel a bit overwhelming," Nexhan said and stepped forward.

A huge room, lined with rows of shelves from floor to ceiling with pottery to jewelry, clothing and trinkets, whole suits of armor, opened before Cole. Thick roots spanned the entire ceiling and Cole swore he could see the magic leaking from the roots as glowing green strands of silk dangled from the tree's system.

"Are these seeds?" Cole asked, poking a fat sack.

"Yes. We grow the plants every year. It's what we make our rune ink from." Nexhan smiled.

Cole nodded and spanned the shelves. He cocked an eyebrow and asked, "Hershey's chocolate bars?"

Nexhan laughed. "Nakoda tells me that Hihano has to hide his chocolate, as Cherchi is apt to devour it."

Cole grinned and shook his head. Something glittered off to the side, catching his attention.

Nexhan must have caught it too, because he warned, "Careful with that. Its name is *Shinami'etahou*, the Death Bringer. It was once in the possession a very powerful shaman—Storm's father. It holds the same magic as *Akumai'ai*, so don't touch it. In fact, it probably wouldn't *like* you to touch it. Its magic is a little dark."

Cole nodded. "I won't. I just want to look at it."

He walked up to the object of his fascination. The sword lay quietly in its scabbard, the hilt and handle carved of bone, still white even after all these years. It seemed to swirl with blackness—that was until he made out the images of black birds. *Crows*. He heard Nexhan call his name, but he was too enthralled with the weapon. He got closer, if only to admire its beauty when he realized the images of crows weren't painted or carved. They were inlaid in the sword itself with magic and they seemed to dance as if the sword were the very sky. The distant clatter of crows flying through the night sky reeled him in. A blue light leaked out from inside the scabbard, the blade aglow and strands of magic unfurled, wrapping their web thin fingers around him. He came closer and reached a hand out to touch it.

"Cole!" Nexhan grabbed his wrist and yanked him away. "I said don't touch it!"

"I wasn't... I mean, at least... I didn't realize what I was doing," Cole stumbled to explain.

The Rune Fang looked at him suspiciously. "It called to you?"

Cole shrugged. "I don't know. I just thought it was beautiful and wanted to get a closer look. The way the birds danced on it was —"

"Birds?"

Cole looked at the sword. The crows were silent, motionless. "The crows? On the pommel. They aren't moving now."

"What crows?" Nexhan asked suspiciously.

"You don't see them?" he asked, aghast. Was he hallucinating now? He was sure the buzz from the pipe weed had worn off.

Nexhan sighed wearily and let Cole go. "I didn't realize that this place might be dangerous to you. With the magic awakening in your presence, things long asleep might too. Come, let us leave."

Cole didn't say anything. He felt the urge to take the blade because... Well, because he *wanted* it. But that was stupid. Now that he knew how to get down here and where it was, he was sure he could slip in unnoticed. *What? I'm thinking of stealing now?* Bonking himself in the head, he followed Nexhan out of the room. The light of the sconces slowly died as they left and the slam of a door startled Cole.

"You said the sword belonged to a shaman. If it called to me, does that make me...?"

"Maybe, but I don't think you're shaman. I've known a few in my time and you don't feel like one. Besides, Donoma didn't recognize you as shaman, either, and he has a talent for recognizing gifts."

"Donoma is a shaman?" Cole asked, intrigued.

"No, not exactly. He is something much rarer," Nexhan explained then turned suddenly. "Swear to me you won't tell anyone what I'm about to reveal. He doesn't like for many to know his true nature."

Cole shrugged. "I swear."

Nexhan studied him for a moment. "I'm going to hold you to that, and I think the magic will too. Donoma is an empath."

"What's that?" Cole scowled.

"Empaths are the Goddess Callari's blessed. They sense the emotions of others and even manipulate one's feelings. Our history is peppered with them and Donoma is the only empath I am aware of who still lives," Nexhan explained.

"That sounds pretty neat," he said.

"Not necessarily." Nexhan looked at him grimly. "Because of their abilities, empaths are extremely sensitive to emotions. It's why Donoma seems so level, because he has to be careful to regulate the energies and not let the emotions of others influence his own. If you were paying attention tonight, you would have noticed that he seemed...extremely happy. That's because he was absorbing the emotions of everyone present."

"He did seem a little cheery. I thought maybe he had gotten into some pipe weed. So if someone is extremely upset, will he get all weepy?" Cole poked.

Nexhan sighed at Cole's tease. "Generally, no. But if you have a whole group of people in the grip of immense sorrow, it could drive an empath mad. I nearly witnessed…" He quickly closed his mouth and squeezed his eyes shut. Cole thought he was going to be shut out again, but to his surprise, the man spoke quickly. "I once watched an empath nearly break. It's not pretty and I never want to see it again."

Cole absorbed that for a moment. "Well, I guess we can cross shaman, Earth-Touched and empath off the list of what I could be. I mean, from Cherchi's enthusiasm alone, I should be singing and clicking my heels."

Nexhan boomed with laughter and slung an arm around Cole's shoulders. "Come on, cub."

"This Goddess Callari? I've heard the name mentioned a few times around the campfire. Who is she?" Cole inquired, ignoring the Rune Fang's jab.

"The Goddess Callari is part of The Three. We don't really know what they are. The texts that we have saved only mention names and not a whole lot more. Callari governs the energies emitted from the emotions of all living things. Then there is the Lore Keeper who is said to possess all the knowledge in the universe. And lastly…The Gray Man. During my time with the Loupen, I learned of the Annunaki. It is said the three Annunaki came down to show the Loupen how to balance their positive and negative halves. I think the Annunaki are the same as The Three."

Cole absorbed that information and walked in silence when he noticed they were going deeper into the ground.

"Ah, here we are." Nexhan smiled. He did some of his voodoo and the door opened. "There isn't as many magical things in here, so you should be fine."

"*Should* be." Cole sighed. He followed Nexhan's dark shape. The air wasn't as clear here, a thin musty scent occupying the room. He saw the shapes of bookshelves filled with tomes of all sizes and thickness. "Is this the library?"

"Yes," Nexhan said. "We use a lot of magic to preserve the tomes. Some of the scrolls originating from Shairobi were scribed on sturdy paper, but time has a tendency to age everything."

Cole heard the clicking of stones before a soft, buttery light flared. He squinted for a moment as his eyes adjusted. Nexhan set a candle down on a desk, his attention solely on his task. The light spread slowly until the room was illuminated. The library was almost as spacious as the treasure room, but writing desks and stacks of books, maps and other literary things occupied most of the nearby area.

"Come sit here with me, Cole," Nexhan ordered. "You might find this interesting. I asked Nakoda to look into your family line."

Cole obeyed, coming up beside Nexhan, who took a seat. A very large, thick leather-bound tome lay opened and bookmarked on the desk. He peered closer but before he could read a word, the Rune Fang pulled him into his lap.

"Only one chair, sorry," Nexhan said, his tone filled with wicked intent.

"That's okay. I could sit on you all day," Cole teased, ignoring the fact that there was another chair buried in a corner.

Nexhan chuckled softly, clearly liking that idea. "Here. Look."

They leaned in together. Nexhan pointed to the top of the page where ancient symbols headed a diagram.

Cole said, "I know that symbol. It's my family line."

"Yup. Starting with Kateesha Nicoyla and her mate, Nokan, who were the first Nicoyla to arrive from Shairobi, along with their three daughters and two sons," Nexhan said.

"Whoa," Cole mouthed as he traced the family paths. They branched out, detailing mates and progeny until they stopped abruptly. "This is really something. But how come the records stopped about two thousand years ago?"

Nexhan sat quietly for a moment as he studied the chart. "My father told me that shifters of all species would come here to study and that our village was like a port where shifters could connect with one another. I can only assume that these records are the result of a collective effort. I'm sure most clans do their own record keeping nowadays."

Cole met his gaze and smiled. "Let's see your line."

"Okay," the male conceded and closed the book carefully. It must have been a foot thick. "Here. See the symbols? There's mine."

Cole followed Nexhan's line of sight and was surprised to find little tabs of leather etched with symbols of shifter species. He helped Nexhan open the book and they skimmed through the different Rune Fang families until Nexhan pointed at the symbol for his family name.

"I can't read it," Cole admitted.

"Rikonosh. The 'SH' is almost silent, barely sounded out. At least that is how I was told it is pronounced in *Qui'nodo'nai*." He shrugged. "Supposedly, Nosh means shield, and 'Riko' is person or being. So…one who carries a shield. Riknah is the word for guardian. It's very close to my family name."

"My father told me Nicoyla means 'cat with a white pelt' — or something like that," Cole said. "If you ask me, it doesn't make any sense. What does your first name translate to?"

Nexhan made a strange sound then sighed and sat back against the chair. His cheeks turned pink. "I loved my parents, but they must have been high on pipe weed when they named me."

Cole grinned. "Come on. I promise I won't laugh."

Nexhan glared at Cole for a second then sighed. "Han can mean either bright or… happy, depending on its context. Nexa is the word to describe something that is extreme or 'full of'."

Cole tried to cover the snort that bubbled up. "So, wait… One who is full of happiness?" He couldn't help but to erupt in laughter. "That's not you at all!"

Nexhan sighed disgustedly while Cole tried to get a hold of himself.

"I assume all parents think their cubs are little balls of happiness and don't think about what they might turn out to be as they grow up." Nexhan growled. "And you said you wouldn't laugh."

Cole hiccupped. "Sorry. I can't help it."

"Well," — Nexhan humphed — "as far as I'm concerned, *'one who is full of happiness'* isn't as bad as *'plump cheeks'*."

Shocked, Cole studied him for a moment. "What do you mean?"

Smirking, Nexhan said, "If my translation is right, 'Col', ample in size, and 'ban', face."

Cole blinked at the male. He was kidding, wasn't he? "You're just saying that because you're mad that I laughed."

Nexhan shrugged nonchalantly. "I'm pretty good with translations. Donoma taught me well. Not as good as Nakoda, though, I suppose I could ask him to verify it."

Grinding his molars, Cole looked away suddenly mortified. *Plump cheeks?* What the hell were his parents thinking? He moved to get up from Nexhan's lap, but the man wrapped his arms around Cole's waist.

"You are going to pout now?" he teased. "I happened to find the name quite accurate."

Cole growled as his face heated. "I can't believe my parents would give me such an ego-smashing name!"

Nexhan boomed with laughter. "I like it."

"Well, I don't!" He grumbled, giving up on trying getting away from the Rune Fang.

Nexhan purred against Cole's shoulder and nipped at the skin, sending chills up his spine. He lazily licked a path up Cole's neck and he couldn't help but to melt in the man's embrace.

"Don't tell anyone, especially my brother. It's embarrassing," Cole whispered.

Nexhan chuckled darkly. "I'm just teasing, Cole. A more accurate translation would be *'fair features'*. I still hold to my opinion, however. Your name suits you."

Cole growled weakly at Nexhan but relief flooded him. He was glad he didn't have such a cheesy name after all.

"Although..." Nexhan laughed and pushed Cole over the desk, landing a hard spank on his ass. "You do have plump cheeks."

"Ow!" Cole laughed as Nexhan tried to turn him over his knee, but he wasn't about to let the Rune Fang get the better of him. He twisted in his lover's hold and wrapped his legs around Nexhan's hips. They met eye to eye and Cole smirked, "Got you."

Nexhan growled low in his throat. "Mmm, so you do. What do you plan to do with me?"

Cole grinned impishly and took Nexhan's lips, kissing him slow and deep. Nexhan moaned softly against him and gripped Cole's ass tightly. Cole threw his weight down when Nexhan tried to take command. The male purred against Cole's lips, but he refused to budge. Cole sucked Nexhan's tongue in a fucking motion.

Breaking off, Nexhan cocked a playful eyebrow. He began tickling Cole and Cole tried to hold back his laughter, but it was too much. As soon as Cole loosened his hold, Nexhan set into action, flipping Cole over and pressing him against the table. A hard palm came down on Cole's ass and he laughed uproariously, trying to get free from the biting stings. He felt the Rune Fang back off momentarily but was back on him right away, that crafty tongue licking its way up Cole's back. Nexhan gripped at Cole's ass roughly and Cole sighed in pleasure, letting himself relax.

Cole moaned as Nexhan took his time, savoring the skin of Cole's back, the male's breath hot against his flesh. Cole's fingers sought purchase on the edges of the table Nexhan pressed him farther down. He gasped when the shifter gripped his cock through his jeans. He wasn't going anywhere anytime soon. Hell, he didn't want to. Nexhan thrust against him, the bulge in the Cole's jeans evident, and Cole bumped his head on the giant book in the process. When he moved to close and set it aside so it wasn't damaged, something caught his eye.

"Nex," he croaked, trying to concentrate through the fog of passion.

"What do you want? Tell me," Nexhan purred against his ear. "Do you want me to fuck you like this, hmm? Or do you want my tongue?"

"Look at this," Cole said.

"I know," he whispered, rubbing Cole's erection.

Cole groaned but was able to find his voice. "No, I mean *look*."

Nexhan came up behind him and peered over his shoulder. "You want to read now?"

Cole pointed to the Rune Fang symbol printed on the top of the page.

"Yeah, that's me. What about it?" Nexhan asked, a bit agitated.

"I've seen it before," Cole said, flipping the pages back to the cougar lines. He felt Nexhan press closer to him, the man's obviously curiosity peeked. "Here it is."

The top of the page was marked with the cougar symbol just above the Nicoyla line. He pointed to the little box that connected to one of the first cougars to arrive and pointed at his mate. "Why is the Rune Fang symbol next to this dude's mate's name?"

Nexhan backed off and stood up. "Huh. Good question."

Chapter Ten

Nexhan took a deep breath, pulling in the scents of the forest deep into his lungs. The crisp smell of the redwood sap, the pungent weeds, the sweet smell of wildflowers — it all cleansed him. A familiar, faint scent caught his attention and a silly smile crept upon his face.

He followed the trail, tasted the pheromones. His cat twitched its tail and perked its ears, eager for the hunt's reward. Anticipation flowed through his veins, heightening his senses. His nostrils flared as the scent intensified and his groin grew heavy. The object of his fascination was just around one giant tree… He could feel it.

Nexhan peeked around the bark and let a tender smile spread across his face.

The male leaned against a sequoia, his eyes looking up into the sky wistfully. His sandy-brown hair hung long and loose around his face. Suddenly, his mouth lifted in a grin. He looked at Nexhan and smiled a smile only meant for one person. "Hey there, big boy."

Nexhan's insides tumbled in excitement as the man he loved looked at him with those luminescent eyes. They held nothing but promise and life, as if the very world was held in those orbs.

The male rose to his feet, his naked body gloriously displayed. His eyes crinkled in the corners. "You need to stop coming here. You have to start looking forward, not back. I'm not here anymore, Nex."

Something unpleasant jumped inside Nexhan. Fear enveloped him. "What do you mean?"

Slowly, the man began to fade, but his smile persisted.

"Don't go! Don't leave me!" Nexhan pleaded, rushing to his lover. He reached out, but Inari was gone, evaporated into the very air.

Nexhan shot up, gasping for breath. It took him a second to realize he was in the library, deep underground, and not in the forest. It had been a dream—a nightmare. Frustration and pain filled him. He'd always let himself dream to medicate his pain, but now it had become tainted. Why? He was sure it had to do with the discovery he'd made last night. Apparently, cross-shifter reproduction was a very real possibility. Long after they'd made love and Cole had fallen asleep on the floor, Nexhan read late into the night. He had discovered that a Rune Fang and a cougar had mated, producing several halfling cubs. Shifters had always thought this an impossibility, but here was proof in his very hands.

He was getting too close to Cole and every second he grew further away from Inari. How could he betray him so easily? He'd never been so confounded. *It's just sex, just shared pleasure. Nothing more.*

Liar.

Blindly, Nexhan reached for Cole, needing comfort, even if the cougar was the source of his confusion, but the male was not there. He scanned around. The candle had burned to its base and died a long time ago. He thought that the cougar might be reading, but there was no one in the room but him.

Maybe that's a good thing. He didn't want Cole to see him so shaken. Slowly, he lay back down and took several deep breaths to still his nerves. The air was thick with the scent of earth, roots and soil, more than it had ever been before. He was surrounded by magic still humming from interacting with Cole.

Nexhan stretched then got to his feet and stepped into his pants, drawing them up over his legs and hips. He made his way up the tunnels, listening to the whispers of the earth. He wasn't sure what they were saying, but he got the impression they were lonely. How strange and intriguing. Reluctantly, he pressed his palm against the stone and closed his eyes. The magic touched him softly, welcoming him with a handshake, but didn't react to his presence. It wasn't *him* it wanted.

He quickly sealed the entrance to the tunnel and set off to find Cole. It wasn't very hard. The man's scent was branded into his brain and his presence was like a beacon. Maybe it was the trace amount of blood Nexhan had taken into his body when he'd licked the cougar's wound. That made sense. He refused to think it was anything else.

Nexhan found Cole on the outskirts of the clearing, sitting on a fallen log, just staring at the sky with a wistful expression. Nexhan ignored the shutter of *deja vu*.

"Hey," Cole said when he noticed Nexhan. "You were pretty tired so I figured I'd let you sleep. You even missed first meal. Were you up late?"

"I did a lot of reading. Discovered something interesting," Nexhan said, sitting next to the cougar.

"Yeah? What's that?" he asked, bumping Nexhan with his body playfully.

"Apparently your discovery establishes that a Rune Fang and a cougar mated and had three daughters and four sons," Nexhan announced, slapping the man on the thigh.

"No shit? I didn't think we could cross breed?" he stated, wide-eyed.

"Neither did I," Nexhan conceded.

Cole thought for a moment, pursing his lips. "Do you know of anyone who's ever tried?"

"No. I plan to ask Donoma about that later," he said. "You know, this could be huge."

"So, I have a half-breed in my line?" Cole asked astonished.

Nexhan hadn't thought about that. He'd been so busy deciphering the symbols and matching up everything that he'd forgotten about whose line it was. Nexhan looked at Cole and blinked. "Wow. I'll have to do more research, but you could be the direct descendant of a halfling."

"That's so fucking cool!" Cole conceded. "Maybe that's why I'm so tall. And why I have weirdo eyes... I know Rune Fangs have a tendency for strange colors." Then he got up and made a show of flexing his muscles.

"Whoa there, beefy." Nexhan laughed. "You're getting a little ahead of yourself. Even if that is the case, hundreds of generations have come before you, each burying the Rune Fang gene."

Cole smiled. "Yeah, but didn't you say something about things long lying dormant?"

Nexhan scratched his ear. "True, that."

Sitting beside Nexhan again, Cole beamed. "Maybe that's why I'm so messed up. Not being able to speak through the earth and... I mean, if I have both cougar and Rune Fang energies, then they could be conflicting, scrambling things, you know?" He took a deep breath then said solemnly, "It would be such a relief to know that it's not my fault I'm a klutz."

Nexhan took Cole's chin in his hand and planted a quick kiss on his lips. "You're not messed up. But, that is a very good assessment. You just might be onto something."

Cole smiled shyly and they sat there in silence for a while, admiring the day and watching the birds fly by. A big black bear moseyed into the clearing and Cole offered the animal a piece of honey candy. The creature took it without hesitation and devoured it. Nexhan patted the bear on the flank and it lazily wandered off toward the village, probably to beg for more free treats.

"You want to know what I think?" Cole asked unexpectedly as he gazed into the cloudless sky. His gorgeous violet eyes refracted the light, setting them aglow.

Nexhan wanted to pull him into his arms and never let him go. Familiarity stung him. How many times had he and Inari spent days like this together?

"I think maybe cross-breeding wasn't so rare in Shairobi. Maybe there weren't clans of tigers or wolves or raptors but just *a* clan of every imaginable species united with big Momma leading us." He sighed. "For some reason or another, we separated ourselves, formed our own clans. Maybe that's our downfall." He looked tenderly at Nexhan. "I mean, no offense, but you're not exactly flourishing here in the middle of nowhere."

A stir of anger at the cougar's words gripped Nexhan, but it passed and he quickly saw Cole's logic. It made sense like the earth and sky made sense. A newfound respect for the young man gripped Nexhan.

"Just look at Mewah and Caroline—Rune Fang and human. Donoma said in his story that we came here to watch over humanity and protect them from Darkness, but what if we were meant for more? Hell, what if mates are forever living in separation because of our segregation?" Cole shrugged. "I dunno, just a weird idea."

Nexhan didn't know what to say, so he just stared at the grasses at his feet. Cole's idea was both astonishing and inconceivable. It was scary and yet brought hope to those like his clan. What if their mates were out there somewhere in the world, waiting, wondering? *What if Inari wasn't my true mate?*

"Just curious? Who's Inari?" Cole asked.

Fear and outrage gripped Nexhan. He snarled, "What do you know of Inari?

"Geez, I was just asking. You kept muttering that name in your sleep last night," Cole said.

Nexhan got to his feet and began pacing back and forth. He shouldn't be surprised. He'd dreamed of Inari often and he was sure he'd called for his lost lover in his sleep. But having Cole know about the man broke something inside him. He couldn't describe it. Inari had been *his*. His first and *only* love— his intended *mate*. And all that was left of the male was Nexhan's memories. Inari's name on Cole's lips was sacrilege!

"Nex? What's wrong?" Cole asked. When he didn't get a response, he got up. "Sorry. I didn't mean to upset you. I was just curious."

"It's none of your business!" Nexhan snapped, as he tried to cover his fear with anger. How dare Cole try to replace his beloved Inari?

Cole's expression grew heated. "No, maybe not. Doesn't give you the right to act like an asshole, though."

That stopped Nexhan. How dare this cub treat him with such disrespect? He glowered at the male. "Excuse me?"

"I knew something was bothering you, but you refused to tell me, refused to extend the same courtesy I have to you. Am I not trustworthy?" He growled.

"I've told you before," he seethed, "I'll not talk about it!"

"You've told me *nothing*!" Cole snapped back. "No wait... I get it. I'm not good enough to know. Not good enough, period."

Nexhan waved him off. "Don't play the pity card. It's getting old."

Flabbergasted, Cole stared at him. "Pity? I've told you I don't want your pity, you arrogant asshole! I thought you understood, now more than ever. Was that just bullshit you were spewing earlier to get me to trust you so I'd tell you everything? I do trust you, by the way. Isn't that part of being lovers?"

Lovers. That world scared the shit out of Nexhan. No. They couldn't be lovers. His true love had only ever been Inari. He'd never abandon his true-mate for a scamp of a cougar. He asked, baffled, "Lovers? Is that what you thought?"

Cole blinked. "I thought—"

"You thought wrong," Nexhan said, emotionless, though his heart ached. He supposed it had to come to this. "Whatever gave you the idea that it was more than sex?"

Cole worked his jaw, but nothing came out of his mouth. His big violet eyes shone brightly, his expression falling as realization hit him. "Just a...fuck?"

"I never meant to lead you on." Nexhan sighed ruefully.

Cole glared, his youthful mask of arrogance back. "No, of course not. Silly me."

"You have to understand, Cole. My species is on the brink of extinction. If it's possible for a Rune Fang and a human to procreate successfully, then that is my path. It would be different if it was a shifter, but a human woman would not understand the concept of a breed-mate," he said, his throat burning.

Cole sputtered a laugh. "So this was just some nookie while you wait for the perfect girl to come along? You're serious?" He gnashed his teeth. "You're a fucking hypocrite!"

Hypocrite. That word stung him. "You speak to me like that again and you won't like the consequence." Nexhan saw and felt the cougar's hurt keenly and it was tearing him apart inside. He hadn't wanted it to end like this—not with all the shouting and crushed feelings. "Cole—"

"Don't touch me!" Cole yelled and pushed up against Nexhan's shoulder.

Nexhan barely had time to register the fact that his feet had left the ground and he was soaring through the air. He slammed into the ground and slid several feet, his breath punching out of his chest. Where the hell had that immense strength some from? He blinked at Cole.

Cole's shocked expression quickly evaporated as a tear slid down his flushed cheek. He wiped it away and looked at it, knitting his brows in confusion. He tossed one last longing glance at Nexhan before rushing off toward the village. Nexhan jumped to his feet and went after him. It couldn't end like this. He's said the wrong things in the wrong way! He had to make it right! He touched Cole's shoulder, but the male spun around, his face wet with angry tears.

"Fuck off!" He growled then gasped, his attention on something behind Nexhan. "Shit!"

Nexhan followed Cole's line of sight to where Nashuk had just entered the clearing. He clutched his hand to his abdomen, and blood stained his clothes, his face a mask of desperation as he screamed for aid. Nexhan and Cole didn't stop to ponder the scene — they took off running for the male. Just as Nexhan reached Nashuk, he collapsed, falling into Nexhan's arms.

"*Mi'wisa!*" Nashuk croaked through chapped lips. "Kaga. Cherchi bade me to return to the village for help. He said he could outrun them. I didn't want to leave him."

Nexhan hushed his brother, moving the bloody locks of hair from his eyes. "It's okay. I've got you."

Cole came next to Nashuk and touched him gently. Nexhan pushed him away, not in anger, but desperation. "Go get help!"

Cole raced toward the village.

"Please... I didn't want to leave him..." Nashuk whispered over and over.

Nexhan caressed his brother gingerly, while reassuring him with gentle words. His wounds were nasty and messy, but not fatal. In fact, they looked to be healing quite well already. Within the span of a few moments, shouts of anger and worry went up from the village and the heavy footfalls of large shifters trotted across the clearing.

Cole was the first to reach him when he returned, along with Storm.

Storm fell to his knees and looked Nashuk over. His brows knitted for a second as if he didn't understand something then he said, "He will be fine."

The rest of the group surrounded Nexhan, who handed an unconscious Nashuk off to Storm. Standing tall, Nexhan boomed, "I want Mewah and his mate and cub protected at all times. Storm will come with us, in case Cherchi needs aid." He directed some of his brothers to return to the village with Nashuk. "We will not tolerate this attack and we will not stop until every last Kaga is slain!"

Donoma stepped forward, along with his brother. "We will fly overhead and be your eyes."

Nexhan nodded then punched his fist in the air, eliciting shouts from his brothers. Broan shifted into his cat form with a proclaiming roar that let their enemies know pain was on its way.

"What about me?" Cole asked.

"Go back to the village. This is what we were made for. This isn't your fight," Nexhan said.

"But, I can help," Cole refuted.

"Damn it, Cole! Stop being a cub and do as you're told!" Nexhan snapped then turned and shifted with a burst of angry light. He didn't stay long enough to see the cougar's expression. His heart couldn't handle it. He hadn't meant to berate the male like that, but he was scared for Cherchi and still humming from his confrontation with Cole. They were *not* lovers. They *couldn't* be. His heart solely belonged to Inari.

Inari is dead.

Then my heart is too, and I will have no other.

He ran into the woods, his brothers behind him as their roars echoed through the trees. Above them, the whooping cries of the hawks followed, cheering them on. Saliva flowed freely and his claws dug into the dirt. Nexhan was frenzied, pissed at what had just happened, and at Cole. Using his confusion and longing for Cole as an accelerant, he vowed to leave not one scrap of Kaga alive.

* * * *

'This isn't your fight.'

The fuck it wasn't. The Rune Fangs had been nothing but kind to him and he'd be damned if he was just going to sit around and not do shit to help them. And hell, he wanted to scream at Nexhan that the desire to protect didn't make him a cub!

Cole growled to himself as he watched Nexhan and the other cats rush into the forest while the hawks soared overhead. Tension hung thick in the air, along with fear. Cole spun around to help the bears and Kale carry Nashuk into a cabin where Mewah was with Caroline and Adam. Cole's first goal was to secure the perimeter, make sure everyone would remain safe. One of the bears had already shifted, the massive ball of fur and claws pacing around the door, ready to shred any threat that got too close.

"Fear not. My brother has a fierce temper and won't let anything through that door," one of the female bears said.

Cole nodded at her politely.

"His wounds aren't serious," the bear shaman said, removing some pungent herbs from a bag.

"I'm fine," Nashuk gasped. "Please... Help Cherchi."

The bear shaman smiled. "All is well. Your brothers will bring him back sound. I'm sure."

Cole bit his lip. Mewah was in the corner with Caroline and the baby, his posture tense. Everything was locked down. All the inhabitants not on the hunt for Kaga were in the main lodge with a wall of fur guarding the door. Talon was in the corner, leaning against the wall, looking cool and collected. He raised his eyebrows in expectancy, as if waiting for Cole to do something.

Cole decided he wasn't needed here.

"Where are you going?" Kale barked.

"I'm not sitting here on my ass," Cole yelled back as he burst out the door.

"Let them handle it!" he snarled, catching up to Cole.

Cole ignored him and beat feet over to Nexhan's cabin.

"Cole! Are you listening to me?" Kale snapped.

Cole avoided his brother's grasp and turned on him. "I have to do this!"

"Why?" Kale asked, aghast.

"It's just something I have to do." *Because I'm not a cub. I'm a man and I'm capable of defending those I care about.* He pushed the door open and grabbed *Akumai'ai* and a quiver of arrows. His brother wouldn't understand. Hell, even *he* didn't understand. It was as if someone had taken control of his motor functions and was walking him into battle. Besides, he wasn't going to sit on his ass like a pussy.

Kale blinked at Cole, who sighed and pulled his brother close, patting him on the back. "I'll be fine."

He didn't give Kale a chance to respond. He raced for the forest, his heart pounding so hard against his ribcage he thought it might escape, but he'd made up his mind. He knew his determination was more than just need to protect the Rune Fangs. He had something to prove to Nexhan. He wasn't just a klutz or a helpless child—he was more. He was worthy of the Rune Fang leader. That, and he was scared the male might get hurt. Despite their argument, he didn't want anything bad to happen to Nexhan.

He broke through the young trees and used his sense of smell to lead him. His mind picked up the faint whispers the clan was using to communicate with one another and for once, he was glad he couldn't relay his own thoughts. He didn't want to alert Nexhan to his plan. They were far ahead, but Cole sensed on their agitation. They were hunting and he could almost feel their cat's excitement. He was anxious to catch up with them but was careful to keep an eye out for any Kaga. The last thing he wanted to do was become a liability. Maybe he had been too hasty in rushing off... Kale had had a point—the Rune Fangs were built to defend, to stand against nasties like the Kaga. He was just a scrawny—

The cougars were once the personal guards of the Mother Goddess. Well, that had to count for something, didn't it?

Don't wimp out now.

The caw of a crow caught his attention. He looked up to see familiar oil-drop eyes staring back at him from a low branch. The beasty blinked at him once then swooped down and made right for Cole. He ducked just in time, but the taloned feet got a good grip on his hair and took off, effectively yanking out a few strands.

Cole batted it away and set into motion, following the bird with a vengeance. He knew he was off course, but something very primal and powerful pulled him. He pumped his legs hard, his feet hitting the turf harder and his breath punched in and out of him until his lungs ached. *Akumai'ai* was pulsating in his hand— it had grown so warm that his palm had begun to sweat. The crow called to him. It hovered just above and in front of him. He didn't realize how fast he was moving, the passing foliage nothing more than a blur. He had become an unstoppable predator, his reflexes honed to perfection, his body a weapon in itself. His fangs punched out of his skull and he felt his cat clawing at him, trying to get out. It was almost surreal, as if he were in a dream or in between two worlds. He hummed as if he were pure energy.

Still, he couldn't shake the feeling that something was guiding him, looking out for him.

A roar went up and Cole skidded to a stop. He sucked in his breath and held it, his ears perked. The forest was so quiet that his own breath sounded loud to his ears, the birds hushed in fear, the animals buried themselves into hidey-holes. He caught the faint rush of water and realized he was near the stream.

The crow landed on his shoulder, sinking its talons into his skin as if urging him to go on. It pecked at his hair gently in a reassuring touch. Cole closed his eyes and concentrated on the energy waves flying back and forth between the Rune Fangs and the hawks. *Two. Water. Help. Cherchi.*

Cole gritted his teeth and burst through the foliage shielding the river. He found himself on a bank, elevated by a dozen or so feet of boulders and washed-up rocks. He gasped as he took in the scene.

Nexhan was leading the attack against a Kaga down the bank of the river, but Cole's attention zoomed in on a vile and dark aura across from his perch. He'd never seen a Kaga before and the demon's presence was petrifying, to say the least. Its body was linear and smooth and oil black, so shiny that it appeared metallic. It reminded Cole of a worm—with limbs. Its head was bullet-shaped with a big maw that perpetually smiled with wicked, dripping fangs. It had no eyes or any other features. Cole couldn't help the fear running through him. The demon emitted some kind of negative energy designed to dishearten its prey.

"Protect! Help!" The words bounced around Cole's mind, the sheer fear and desperation distorting the waves.

Seeing that Nexhan had his catch under control, Cole turned his attention to Nakoda, who was defending Cherchi's limp body just on the other side of the stream. The male snapped and snarled at the demon, as he put his body in front of the fallen Rune Fang. The Kaga wagged its tail, seemingly delighted by the display, but its sights were purely on Cherchi.

Fucking bullies, always want to pick on the weak. He swallowed, unsure what to do. The bow grew warmer against his palm, pleading to be used. Cole's new friend took off from his shoulder, cawing.

"Three! Three!" The hawks cried above.

Cole heard himself cry out as a third Kaga emerged from the trees, its sight set on Nakoda. He tried to alert the male to the danger, but just before the Kaga fell upon the Rune Fang, Donoma swooped down and sunk his lethal talons into the beast's head, pecking for purchase. The vile thing screeched and whipped around violently, shaking Donoma away. The hawk corrected himself in midflight and retreated.

Nexhan and his clan had noticed the appearance of the other Kaga and started for Nakoda, but they'd never make it in time.

Akumai'ai burned Cole and he winced. *Take me up! I am yours!*

Cole completely acted on instinct. He retrieved an arrow, notching it against *Akumai'ai*. He felt the bow's approval. He aimed, focusing in on the third Kaga charging Nakoda. If he could just distract them long enough for Nexhan to reach Nakoda…

Please, please, don't let me miss. He'd made good shots before. He could do it. He had to. But there was always that possibility of failure. *'Will the arrow to where you want it to go. That is part of the magic of Akumai'ai!'*

The crow cawed loudly, cheering him on.

Cole steeled himself against the urgent and distracting energies from the other shifters and took a deep breath. He prayed to whatever gods might be listening and let the drawstring go. Time seemed to slow down as the projectile whistled through the air. He heard his breath rush out, heard the angry snarls of the cats and the whooping cries of the hawks stretched into long drawn out sighs.

The arrow slammed home with brutal force, cutting through the beast's grotesque mouth and knocking it off its feet. A moment of pride filled Cole as he landed the perfect shot. The creature squirmed and squealed, clawing at the arrow protruding from its jaws.

Nakoda quickly recovered and resumed his protective stance, the fur on his neck standing up.

Relief flooded Cole and he found himself smiling dumbly at his newfound skill. But Cole hadn't thought of the possibility that the Kaga might turn on him. Seeing that its friend was momentarily incapacitated, the second demon abandoned Nakoda and made for Cole, snapping and snarling brutal-looking teeth that dripped with dirty saliva.

Cole froze and he heard Nexhan's frantic pleas in his head. He had just become the liability he had hoped to avoid. The fight-or-flight response kicked in and his first instinct was to run, but for some reason his feet wouldn't move. He clutched *Akumai'ai* tightly, trusting the magic in the bow, prepared to use it as a club to protect himself. But the Kaga skidded to a stop inches from him. The thing's faceless maw relaxed and it backed away reluctantly. This close and personal, the energy the thing was emitting made Cole want to puke from revulsion, but... Cole thought he sensed fear. That was impossible! Kaga were pure evil. They didn't know fear.

One moment the creature was there, the next a mass of fur and foot-long fangs enveloped it. The clan fell upon it, not wasting a second, tearing it limb from limb. Stunned, Cole watched as Nexhan locked his fangs into the beast's head and quickly snapped its neck, twisting and pulling until separating its grotesque head from its body. There was something very primal and awesome watching the Rune Fang do what he was made for. Black blood spilled everywhere and the demon fell to the ground in a tangle of meat and torn flesh. It quickly deflated and turned into a gooey, oily mess, staining the ground as the evil sank into the earth.

Cole swallowed hard. Everything came to him in a rush. Had he really just landed the perfect shot and somehow scared a demon shitless? He glanced behind him, expecting to see something bigger and badder than the Kaga, but nothing was there other than the foliage—and the crow watching from its perch. It blinked at him from a branch, its head cocked in an inquisitive way, waiting for Cole to do something interesting. Cole felt himself zone out, felt his body being pulled between two realities. He shook his head and pinched his eyes.

He homed in on the Kaga that had an arrow in its head. The beast was recovering. Cole felt its anger and disorientation. Repulsion filled him, along with rage. He had to finish the job.

He moved toward the Kaga as it tried to crawl to Nakoda, who was faithfully acting as bodyguard to Cherchi. Cole walked... Reached out his hand... He wasn't sure why...

Finish it! Rid these lands of its vile presence!

"Cole!" Nexhan screamed for him.

But there was nothing to be done except one thing. He wrapped his fingers around the Kaga's ankle. A wicked chill bit Cole's palm and the slime that coated the demon's skin disgusted every fiber of his being. The thing was an abomination to the very essence of life. Cole felt its desire to destroy, to blacken the earth and devour the light so that its master, Darkness, could rule unhindered. He didn't quite understand its motivation, but it didn't matter. The shithead had threatened his friends and that was a no-no.

The Kaga turned on him and screeched, nasty gray saliva sputtering through needlelike teeth. Cole thought it was going to lunge for him, but it shuttered and fell to the ground, twisting and crying in agony like a dying worm. Its slick body cracked, flaked and floated into the air like ashes. The beast's moans abruptly cut off and all that was left of it was a blackened patch of dust.

Cole looked at his hand, watched the dust slowly blow away from his sullied skin. He felt the Rune Fangs and hawks gathering around him, their auras ripe with confusion and astonishment. He blinked at Nakoda, who watched him closely. He sensed Nexhan's white-hot anger behind him, as if the male was an out of control forest fire, sweeping through and intent on devouring everything in his path. Cole swallowed, unable to look at him. *What the hell just happened?*

The spell was broken when Cherchi made a pained sound. Thank the Goddess he was alive.

Nakoda rushed to his side and Cole followed, hoping there was something he could do. The male lay in bad shape. His neck had been torn apart, the blood still slowly pumping out of the wound, and multiple gashes interrupted the perfect skin of his chest and abdomen. They looked like teeth and claws in search of an anchor as the demons fed.

"Cherchi?" Nakoda whispered.

"Ambushed," Cherchi croaked.

Cole touched the male gently and whispered to Nakoda, "We need to stop the bleeding."

Looking at Cole as if he had grown a set of extra appendages, Nakoda shouted, "Storm! Where is Storm?"

Donoma came forward and pressed a torn piece of cloth to Cherchi's wound. He spoke solemnly, his jaw tight as if he were about to lose control. "This is beyond my specialty."

Nakoda shot to his feet. He called for Storm, his voice hoarse and filled with worry. Cole let the hawk work and looked around. A few Rune Fangs were down the bank of the stream, finishing off what remained of the first Kaga. It wasn't much, to say the least. Cole caught Nexhan's angry glare as the man approached him. Nexhan pushed past him and crouched next to his brother, whispering gentle words.

"Is he...okay?" Cherchi asked weakly. "Tell me... Nashuk... Nashuk!"

"He is fine," Nexhan said and ran his hand through the male's blood-streaked hair. "You did well, brother."

A shuffle to the side caught everyone's attention and Storm burst out of the brush. His eyes flashed with anger and he had a good-sized gash on his abdomen. His coat didn't seem to have fared any better, looking like it had been dragged under a vehicle halfway across the continent. He made his way quickly over to Cherchi and examined the wound.

"Is he going to be okay too?" Cole asked.

Nexhan quickly spun on him, his body tense. His normally bright, golden eyes darkened. "I told you to stay in the village!"

Swallowing hard, Cole stood his ground and motioned at Nakoda. "It's a good thing I didn't."

Stepping forward, Nexhan snarled, "You could have been killed!"

Nakoda approached and placed a gentle hand on Nexhan's shoulder, "*Mi'wisa*, now isn't the time."

Nexhan shrugged him off and came closer, snatching *Akumai'ai* from Cole. "What do you think you were doing? Did you even *think*?"

"Can you please be quiet? You're interrupting my concentration," Storm said with a tone of annoyance.

Cole was aghast at Nexhan's outburst, but before he could reply, his little buddy cawed and swooped in, landing on his shoulder and pecked at Nexhan until he took a step backward. Everyone grew quiet and even Nexhan lost most of his bluster. Cole felt the unspoken words, the feeling of astonishment encircling them. Even the elder hawk seemed at a loss for words. Cole looked to Nexhan with pleading eyes. He said the words in his mind, unable to find the courage to speak them aloud. "*I was scared you'd be hurt. I wanted to help. I don't want to leave things this way between us. Can't you see that?"*

"We need to get him back to the village," Storm said.

Nexhan's gaze turned hard again and he said softly, yet firmly. "This is Rune Fang land and if I tell you to do something, you do it. I won't tolerate that sort of disrespect. If you don't like it, you can get the fuck out."

"*Mi'wisa*, I don't think—" Nakoda started.

Nexhan threw up a hand.

Something cold and hard speared Cole's chest and he had to concentrate to breathe. Did Nexhan really want him gone that badly? Was he really just some needy bitch with the wrong idea? Had the time they'd spent together meant anything at all? The crow on his shoulder beat its wings and cawed loudly, as if voicing its dissatisfaction. Without warning, it took off and attacked Nexhan, plucking at him. Nexhan batted it away.

Whispers of '*Oketa*' filtered through the warriors.

Cole beat back the tears and swung the quiver of arrows off his back. He threw it at Nexhan and said defiantly, "Fine, asshole!"

Nexhan's anger followed him as he turned his back and burst through the foliage. When he was shielded from curious eyes, he picked up his pace and ran, craving the feeling of freedom he'd experienced earlier. But his heart was too heavy. There were no words he could find for what he was feeling. It was like his heart had been scooped out of his chest, leaving a big, gaping hole. He should have known better, known not to trust Nexhan's bullshit advice. He had been content before, believing he was a fuck-up, safe keeping himself closed off from others.

Opening himself up to Nexhan had caused him more pain than he ever thought he'd experience.

The crow cawed overhead. He didn't care, though. He just needed to get far away. He wasn't sure how far he ran, but he raced until his thighs burned and his breath hitched. He fell against a tree, hugging it for support. Sobs clawed at his throat, but he held them back. *No use in crying. It won't fix anything.*

Debris bopped him on the head and he looked up. His friend stared down at him with impossibly kind eyes and he knew no matter how far he'd travel that the little beasty would be there every step of the way. In desperation, he asked, "Why? What did I do wrong?"

The bird just stared with an open beak. It didn't shift its head or caw incessantly at him—only looked. Then it took off, disappearing into the trees. Cole bumped his head up against the tree and tried not to let loose the tears still pricking his eyes. After some time, when the light began to grow dim, he realized something. He wasn't a loser. He had done something good. He had possibly saved a man's life. He had tossed his fears and uncertainties away and didn't deserve the berating he'd received—pride filled him.

"I'm not a fuck-up," he whispered to himself, unable to help the smile from creeping over his lips.

The crunch of a twig caught his attention and Cole turned around. For a moment, disappointment nipped him. Kale smiled. "Hey. There you are."

Cole blinked a few times. "What are you doing here?" He hadn't realized the hour.

"Came to get you," Kale said simply then frowned at the sky. "It's getting late."

"How did you find me?" Cole asked. The sound of a crow cawing in the distance told him all he needed to know. "Never mind. Why are you here?"

"Don't ask silly questions, bro. You think I'm about to let my big brother wander around alone?" he teased.

"Big?" Cole cocked an eyebrow.

"Nakoda told everyone what happened." Kale looked him in the eye. "Everything you did."

He sighed. "I don't really want to talk about it."

"Then let's go home." And with that, Kale tossed an arm around Cole and pulled him to his side.

They walked through the night, arm in arm, Cole needing his brother's support. Kale teased him once or twice, saying he never thought Cole had the balls to do what he'd done, but otherwise, they walked through the forest silently, under the shadow of the crow.

Chapter Eleven

Nexhan blinked, his vision blurry. Where was he?

The forest. He knew these trees, knew the sweet scent of the flowers and moss and – life.

A smile touched his lips. This was the grove he and Cole had miraculously created.

A movement behind the trees caught his attention, but it was nothing more than a white blur. Furrowing his eyebrows, he followed. He weaved in between the giant trunks led by his curiosity of the pale presence. He recognized the purity in it, his shifter magic attracted to the energy. He heard himself call out but no one answered him. Was it Cole playing a game?

He rounded a tree and stopped dead in his tracks. A beautiful white horse, grazing on the grasses, stood in a ribbon of sunlight. Nexhan had never seen such a magnificent beast – its coat, the color of silver clouds, its mane like a spring rainstorm. It nickered and raised its head, perking its ears at Nexhan.

He gasped at the prismatic horn spiraling from its forehead. Deep blue eyes penetrated him, searching his heart and soul.

Without warning, the unicorn took off, trotting into the forest. Nexhan called to it and followed, feeling cumbersome compared to the creature's agility. A flash of white here and there guided his course.

He came to a wild stream and stopped, looking around. Upon the opposite bank, strange trees grew. Their wild limbs twisted and turned, sporting colorful leaves in every conceivable shape. He'd never seen such things, could never have imagined such wildlife.

There! A cloaked figure stood among the trees. Her robes white, pure like the rapids, and golden hair spilled out from her hood. He could not see her face, but she was heavily pregnant.

This couldn't be! Nexhan fell to his knees. "Mother!"

She didn't respond and he was unable to raise his head to look upon her. Did he even deserve to look upon her? This wasn't possible. She couldn't be here. He trembled, unsure what to do.

Then two bare feet came into view. Looking upon them nearly blinded him.

"Would you refuse my gift so easily?" She spoke and her words were like birdsong, insects chirping and wolves howling all at once. He felt as if his ears might bleed. Her power was so great, so immense, he wasn't sure he could stand it, but he recognized that she was angry.

Gift? What gift? Nexhan worked his mouth, but was unable to respond.

Her feet disappeared, but her voice did not, "I brought him back to you and this is how you repay my kindness. How terribly you have wounded me."

Stark fear gripped Nexhan, the cold fingers of disappointment nearly stilling his heart from beating. He didn't know what she was talking about. He had displeased her somehow. How could he make it right?

Something barely touched his hair and he shivered as a current ran through him. She spoke kindly this time.

"Perhaps I have been gone from you too long that you no longer recognize me. This was not my intention."

He swallowed and found his voice. "Please, Mother. I apologize for whatever I have done that has displeased you."

Her tone grew angry again and he thought he'd pass out from the pressure of her fury. "Do not attempt to apologize if you don't know what you are apologizing for!"

A wave of nausea hit him and he tried not to faint. Could you even faint in a dream? Was this a dream? Disgusted with himself, he kept his eyes on the ground. He had failed his people too many times and now apparently the Mother as well. That was unforgivable.

"Do not torture yourself so, my son. I recall a wise man saying that all life is precious. You are indeed precious," she said gently.

Would she touch him? He wanted her to touch him. Something gentle and warm touched the top of his head, the heat soaking into his body and spreading to his limbs.

"The life you have chosen for yourself is not the life I wished you to have. But in this, it is your choice. But you must protect him – he is so very fragile. He needs you more than he knows."

"Who, Mother? Please tell me," Nexhan begged, tears freely falling from his eyes.

She sighed. "Your heart is closed. You must open it. Do not dally long in the realm of the dead, for you are me and I am life. Look inside yourself and I am there – always."

Nexhan blinked up at the thin ribbons of gold streaming down through the sequoias as he came awake peacefully. The dream dimmed and he knew he shouldn't forget it, but it was so strange and unlikely, it couldn't be anything more than a dream, a stir of his subconscious desires. He tried to recall the details, but they faded. It was a nice day, the air mild, but that meant nothing, not here. It could be the coldest day in winter for all he knew.

A dry, shriveled flower petal slapped him in the head and rolled down his body to land on his thigh. He sighed and looked around. The grove he and Cole had created was dying. The leaves were drying out and had become holey from the hungry mouths of insects. The flowers were all but gone, their heavy bulbs sagged as the petals fell off one by one. The once thick and lush moss was nothing more than thin, brittle flakes on the trees and vines hung from branches like dead snakes, defenseless against hungry things looking to recycle them. He'd tried to tend to the garden, tried to water the plants and care for them, but there was no more life here, just impending death.

And it was his fault. *I was terrified.* It scared him that he had come so close to losing his heart all over again. But no matter what excuse he came up with, it didn't make up for the way he had treated Cole. And every day that passed without seeing the male, Nexhan fell deeper into a dark realm where the hot rays of the summer sun could not touch him. Even his brothers were upset with him, though none would admit it. He keenly felt their disapproval and that hurt him to know they were disappointed. And Talon, that strange eagle, had scowled at him continuously all week.

Nexhan's only consolation was that Cole was back with his clan. Kale had sent word that they were both safe back with their family. Apparently, Cole had made directly for his home after their confrontation. It didn't surprise him that Kale had disappeared upon hearing the news.

Confrontation. Hell, Cole had practically told Nexhan that he loved him—or at least cared deeply for him—and what had Nexhan done? Dismissed the male's feelings then belittled him in front of everyone. The fact that Cole might love Nexhan warmed him. *Lovers.* But then that all too familiar cold dread filled him. He knew that for his own good he had to learn to let go. *Let Inari go.*

He felt worthless. He didn't deserve to be clan leader.

Nexhan sighed and bumped his head against the tree. The world around him spun before everything became clear again. He'd lost count of how many times he'd nearly broken out into a run toward the cougar's village, intent on apologizing to Cole. It had not been his intention to hurt the man. At the time, his logic had seemed sound. Find a human mate to breed with and… What? *Deny who I am?* Cole had been right. Nexhan was deluding himself. He was a hypocrite. And apparently, he was a big baby too. Angry and frustrated, he wiped his eyes. What was he supposed to do? He had no idea on how to begin fixing the situation. It was too late and he'd gone too far. He'd said the wrong things, showed his concern in the wrong way.

"*Mi'wisa?*"

Nexhan took a deep breath and shaped himself into the perfect image of a Rune Fang leader. Strong and steady. *Fake.* "Brother."

Nakoda stepped into the clearing, his face gentle, but behind the kind exterior, he knew his friend was still not happy with him.

"How is Cherchi?" Nexhan asked out of reflex.

"He is okay. He was up for a little while, but I'm afraid more than his strength was taken from him," Nakoda said solemnly.

Nexhan closed his eyes tightly and said a silent prayer that it not be the case. If Cherchi's magic had been stolen... Nexhan couldn't finish that thought. The male might as well be dead.

Clearing his throat, Nakoda said, "No one has seen you all day. We were getting a little worried. We thought that maybe you'd —"

Nexhan knew what his friend meant. Nakoda hoped that he'd gone to apologize.

"Well, I figured you'd be here."

"There are some things that can't be fixed," Nexhan said.

"And this is not one of them," Nakoda corrected sternly.

Nexhan got to his feet and looked at his best friend. The male's eyes were kind and considerate and almost made Nexhan want to speak his heart. "I'm not in the mood to talk about it right now."

"No? Then when is the right time, so I can make sure to come back?" Nakoda snapped.

Nexhan sighed wearily. "Please, brother..."

"No. Sitting here and sulking like a cub won't help you or Cole or us!" he said and paused to gauge Nexhan's reaction.

Shocked, Nexhan had never known Nakoda to speak so bluntly to him.

Nakoda's features quickly softened again. "It's time to move on, Nexhan. I know the pain of losing loved ones, but we cannot dwell on it forever. Not only does it affect our own being, it's not good to keep their spirits attached. You have to let Inari go. Some things are not meant to be. You have to accept that you and Inari are not true-mates."

The pain was so sharp that the only thing he could do was attack Nakoda in an attempt to lessen the agony. He swung clumsily, but the male avoided the punch. The force pulled him in and he spun. Nakoda caught him and hugged him close as they crumpled to the ground.

"It's okay, *Mi'wisa!*" Nakoda soothed as Nexhan struggled with his emotions.

"He wanted to bond with me!" Nexhan sobbed, the years of pent-up emotion flooding from him. "But he knew the ramifications, the risks and wouldn't let me! I should have! I should have bonded with him!"

"If that was the way the Mother wished it to be, then it would have been so," Nakoda whispered against his ear. "But you have to accept the possibility that you weren't meant for each other. I know it's hard, but you don't have to suffer. You don't have to forget him, but you can't tie yourself to someone who is no longer here. Just let go."

Nexhan wanted to refute everything his friend was saying, but deep down he knew it was the truth. Many shifters cherished the belief that the Mother Goddess chose their mates at the moment of their creation and they would be born continuously until they finally found each other in life. Nexhan had believed Inari was his true-mate, but Inari had convinced him not to bond with him until peace returned, for fear that the enemy might go after him in attempt to hurt Nexhan.

It had been a courageous sacrifice of the heart and one that had led Nexhan to linger on, forever looking back at what could have been. And until recently, what was supposed to have been. He had loved Inari so deeply. His heart couldn't concede that Inari was not his true-mate. But hearing it spoken for the first time brought a sense of peace... Inari could have been reborn into a new form already, roaming another planet alongside his true-mate... While Nexhan held onto the past. Inari might be sitting in a grove this very second, content and happy with his true-mate...

Of course, he wouldn't remember Nexhan, but he'd be *happy*. That realization cleansed Nexhan in a way he couldn't describe.

'*Look inside yourself and I am there, always.*'

He dug his fingers into the man's arms to pull him closer, needing the comfort. He felt Nakoda's energy. It was warm like sunshine and clean like the wild rapids. He let it soak into him. He wasn't sure how long they lay there, but being in his best friend's presence made him feel better and allowed him to think more clearly.

He patted Nakoda's arm. "I'm okay."

The male reluctantly let him go. When they were on their feet, Nexhan pulled him into a big bear hug and inhaled Nakoda's scent. He patted him on the back then retreated.

"Where are you going?" Nakoda asked, his tone filled with hope.

"I made a promise that I intend to keep," He said simply, and made his way toward *Weynka Le Gai*.

* * * *

Nexhan ran his fingers through his hair that had grown tangled from lack of care. His eyes hurt from all the reading and his brain had turned to mush from the overload of a whole night's work of translating various dialects. Exhausted, he leaned back and watched as the candle flickered softly. Nakoda had stopped by earlier to deliver some tea and cookies that Caroline had baked, to which Hihano had vehemently protested, citing that females were meant to be taken care of, especially new mothers. They had shared a quick laugh at that. Nexhan hadn't missed the expectant looks Nakoda gave him, wondering when —

or if—Nexhan was going to venture to the cougar's village. He didn't give Nakoda an answer and the male left quietly, after recommending some tomes that might help in his search.

Truth was, he was still confounded about what to do with Cole or what their relationship meant. Coming to terms with the truth of something wasn't easy and a part of him balked at the idea of leaving Inari behind and loving another. But somewhere during the countless hours in the library, a voice whispered to him, *"Maybe you already love him."*

That was a terrifying thought. He'd quickly buried it under stacks of books. His mind was set on keeping his promise, though. If there was any way he could possibly be forgiven, then this would be the first step. Unfortunately, he was no closer to discovering what and who Cole was than he was eight hours ago. Frustration and exhaustion sent him snarling and pushing away from the table.

"You were never one for study."

Nexhan blinked and it took him a moment to realize it was just Donoma peeking in, a soft smile on his face.

"I'm getting nowhere! It would help if I knew what I was looking for, but…" He let out a big breath, trying to calm himself. Following the Kaga hunt, the hawk had retreated to a more peaceful place in order to deal with the overload of emotions. Nexhan didn't blame him and he felt a little guilty having added rage to the hawk's cacophony of problems. "Is everything okay? I thought you'd gone away for a while."

Donoma stepped in and closed the door gently behind him. "Everything is okay now. I returned to offer my assistance to Cherchi. I'm afraid to say, I wasn't much use. There are some things even I cannot fix."

Nexhan nodded sullenly. No one should have to go through what Cherchi was experiencing now. Nexhan had visited him a few times and although his body was mostly healed, his spirit was broken. None would speak it, but everyone feared that the Kaga had stolen too much. Nexhan wondered if he'd ever see that bright smile again.

"So, there is another reason why I came back," Donoma said as he took a seat opposite Nexhan. When Nexhan arched an eyebrow, the hawk went on. "In the business of the world, we often find our answers when we take a second to breathe—that moment in time between inhale and exhale. Anyway, I remembered something from when I was just a boy — a story my father read to me from an ancient book." Donoma looked at the mess Nexhan had created. "Do you remember the tomes I gave you for your coming of age?"

Nexhan couldn't help but smile like an idiot. It brought up tender memories. It was one of his proudest moments as a young male and future Gatekeeper. On his fifteenth birthday, Donoma had given him a small collection of old tomes the hawks had possessed since The Coming. He was to guard them, preserve them as his lineage was destined to. He quickly got up from his chair and bit his lip as he looked at the mess.

"Here!" He beamed and moved a stack of books to the side. Donoma came up behind him and watched, his energy radiating light. Nexhan opened the chest and began to pull out tomes bound in carved Totoa hide.

"This one," Donoma said, accepting a small tome engraved with fluid symbols and the emblem of a bird.

"The Messenger and Kaga?" Nexhan translated the raptor's dialect.

Donoma nodded. "My father read it to me once when I was having trouble sleeping. I thought it was perhaps nothing more than a fable, but after witnessing... Well, let us sit and read it together and see what we can learn."

Nexhan joined his friend at the table and they lit a second candle. The tome creaked as they opened it and a familiar magic touched Nexhan. "My very first preservation spell. I'm glad I didn't screw it up."

"I had faith in your abilities as a cub and I still do," the hawk teased playfully.

Nexhan smiled and turned his attention to the book. The language was that of *Qui'nodo'nai,* but the dialect was what set it apart from others. It was very fluid, like water and meant to be spoken with ease and gentleness. The dialect was a representation of the very breeze upon which tiny water drops danced. It wasn't easy to translate, but Donoma had taught him well.

"Let's see... The Coming." The first section talked about the shifters leaving their home world, traveling to earth and how they set up the very first colonies. It was nothing new, but the second section caught both their attentions.

"And seeing the shifters roaming free upon this new land," Nexhan read carefully, "Darkness grew jealous and full of anger. Darkness summoned forth his will to dominate and created Kaga to steal the magic of the shifters."

Donoma nodded. "It's believed that our Mother was very active in Shairobi and wouldn't tolerate the presence of Darkness on her lands, thus shielding us from its ire. However, when we came here, it left us open to attack."

"So, this passage details how the Kaga came into being? Interesting." Nexhan realized that a wealth of information lay hidden in their vaults, protected by years of forgotten tongue and those few who could read them. "Kaga grew great in number and became a plague to both shifter and humanity. Thus the first great war of the new world came about."

"I remember asking my father what Kaga looked like and cringing from the description he gave," Donoma chuckled lightly. "Until I actually saw one, I thought my father had exaggerated his story to frighten me."

Nexhan smiled distantly and flipped the page to the next chapter. "The coming of… *Sha'ique*? Creator?"

"That translation seems sound, but my father called it Life-Binder." Donoma said, studying Nexhan's reaction.

Nexhan furrowed his brows in contemplation. Life-Binder and Creator could mean the same thing, as their meanings were very similar, if not the same. His interest piqued, he went on. "It is said that an eagle soared through the cosmos until he was weary from exhaustion on a quest to seek the aid of the gods against the Kaga. Upon a great battle, the eagle returned. Seeing his kin in peril, he raced to them and in desperation, took a Kaga into his arms to keep it from another then the Kaga was no more, as surely as if it never existed at all."

Swallowing hard, Nexhan frowned at Donoma.

Donoma took the book from him and began reading quickly and fluently, the language easy to him. "Distraught over the death of his brother, the eagle took him in his arms and his tears closed the wounds, cleansing the poison from his body and again the brother's heart beat."

"Resurrection?" Nexhan gaped.

Donoma nodded. "Perhaps… And from this day the eagle was known as *Sha'ique* — Life-Binder. For Mother had touched him and Father walked with him. Moss grew where he stepped, plants awakened to his blood and flowers bloomed upon his seed."

Awareness energized Nexhan as realization crashed into him, nearly knocking his breath out. Everything swirled in front of him until a clear picture formed in his mind. He jumped up and cursed, "Shit!"

"Apt." Donoma chuckled softly.

Nexhan pulled him into a bear hug. "I have to go."

"My friend," the hawk said, stopping Nexhan in his tracks. "There is one thing… A power like this has not been held for thousands of years and I fear that in this world, there are those that would seek to exploit it."

Nexhan took a deep breath and nodded, understanding the wise hawk's words.

'He is so very fragile. He needs you more than he knows…'

Chapter Twelve

Nexhan shared hugs with the cougars. He'd not been to their village for over a hundred years and was surprised to see how modernized it had become. The cougars had established a small township, passing as humans. They even ran a motel for traveling humans, but he had been told the last person to visit had been three years ago. Apparently, a family on vacation had gotten lost.

"One of our females wishes to speak with you, Gatekeeper. Would you spare a few minutes of your time?" an older male named Gris, asked pleasantly. He was clan leader and mayor of their small town.

"Of course. I'd be honored." Nexhan smiled.

Gris had some cubs take Nexhan's meager luggage that consisted of a small traveling satchel containing a pair of clothes and some small gifts, then led him toward the outskirts of the town.

Gris said, "Most of the township is a visage. We still make our homes in the mountains, but many have grown used to the human way of life, especially our cubs. The rest of us, prefer to dwell in more familiar surroundings."

"Dad!" A young cougar of about thirteen came running up. "Ellie wants to know what color blooms for the dining tables!" When the young one spotted Nexhan, his eyes grew big. "Oh... H-hi."

"This is my youngest son, Gray," Gris smiled.

Gray nodded in hello, giving Nexhan a once-over, his disbelief evident.

"I think Mae wanted white. Yes, white," Gris told his son.

The young male rushed off.

Gris laughed. "I feel like a bee with all this running around. But, it's not every day a mating takes place, so I can't complain.

Nexhan conceded. Upon seeing all the decorations and hearing all the talk, he had thought Cole had decided to sacrifice his happiness and mate with the Earth-Touched female. Fear had gripped him them. It had been Nexhan's own ignorance that had led Cole to that idea, but it didn't matter now seeing as this was not the case.

"Forgive me, Guardian, but I did not know a mating ceremony was to happen," he said gingerly, trying to fish for information.

Gris looked stunned for a moment. "Ah, well, I had wondered. We sent out an invitation last night and when you arrived so quickly and alone, I believed you'd left your village before the invitation had arrived."

"This makes sense. I'm sure my brothers will arrive soon to witness the mated pair's ceremony," he said. "However, I've come for a different reason. There is one of yours I must speak with."

Gris stroked his chin as he led Nexhan toward a small cottage nestled against some evergreens. "Bessa mentioned something of this to me. She said that if a Rune Fang arrived, I should direct him to her as soon as possible. She is very gifted, that one."

"Of course, I would be delighted to speak with the Earth-Touched," he said cordially. Truthfully, he was desperate to find Cole and share the news.

"Well..." Gris smiled tenderly. "Here we are. I cannot linger, much to do, but don't be afraid to ask for anything you might need."

Nexhan dipped his head in appreciation then watched for a few moments as the elder cougar made his way back to town. He vaguely wished he'd brought more gifts for the newly mated. He quickly turned his attention to the cottage. He took a deep breath and knocked. The sooner he got this over with, the sooner he could find Cole and do what he needed to do.

"Oh, come in!" a voice yelled from inside.

He peeked in and when he didn't see anyone, stepped inside. It was a cozy little place consisting of a small sitting room with lots of old furniture crafted from woven vines. Something exotic drifted to him.

"Please, come in. I'm in the kitchen!"

Nexhan closed the door behind him and found his way to the kitchen. All he had to do was follow his nose. A delightful older female was at the stove, dressed in a simple, modern summer dress. She was stirring something in a very large pot. She looked up, smiled, quickly dropped the spoon, then wiped her hands on her apron as she came up to Nexhan.

"Gatekeeper. I'm Adrina, Bessa's mom. Welcome to our home. My mate isn't here right now. Like everyone else, he's busy with the preparations." She beamed up at him.

He took her hand and placed a kiss on her knuckles. "I'm happy to be here."

She smiled shyly at him. "Bessa is in the back. She mentioned you might show up today."

"Thank you." He grinned and found the back door.

A large backyard opened up to him with a picnic table off to the side. He found Bessa. She was sitting in the middle of the clearing in a pair of khaki shorts and a tank top, studying some stones arranged in an order only she could understand. She'd tied her hair back in a ponytail. She sat focused, her eyebrows knitted in determined concentration. She raised her arm in the air and made a waving motion. Nexhan supposed that was his cue.

"I think it's going to be a bad winter. The elders said so too." She looked up from the stones and smiled, her blue eyes shining. "Sit with me, Nexhan."

Surprised, he obeyed, folding his legs under him. "You know who I am."

"The stones tell me much." A second passed before she giggled. "Cole told me about you. His words were 'if that asshole shows up, tell him to fuck off'."

He winced. "Guess that doesn't garner me much admiration."

She giggled again, stifling it with her palm. "It's okay. I know his secrets. He is a very passionate male. What he really meant to say is 'send him my way immediately!'" She looked around for a moment and leaned in. "But, don't tell him I told you that."

Nexhan beamed and made a zipping motion across his lips. "Not a word."

"So you came. I'm glad. I wasn't sure you would," she said in all seriousness.

He sighed, unsure what he wanted to tell this young woman. He had a feeling she already knew most of the story.

Bessa made the choice for him. "He can be difficult to read sometimes, because he tries so hard to hide who he really is." She looked at Nexhan then relaxed and leaned back. "He's special. I knew it from the moment we were first introduced. I'd thought I'd hit the jackpot." She sighed ruefully, as if longing for something. She shrugged. "It was clear he just needed a friend, so that's why I asked you to come speak to me right away. This is coming from someone who cares about him. Don't let him push you away. Honestly, you screwed him over and it's going to take a lot for him to get past that. But the stones tell me the match is perfect, more than I've ever seen before."

Speechless, Nexhan could only stare at her. The girl was young but she was incredibly wise. He felt honored having spoken with her. "I hurt him. I'm not sure if he'll forgive me and I'm not sure if I deserve it."

She pursed her lips, pondering his words for a moment then returned to her stones. She placed them in a wooden bowl, shuffled them around a bit then dumped them on the grass. After she touched them gently for a few moments, she looked into his eyes. "He needs you. You can protect him and it's what you were made for. The time was not right back then, but it is now. You've both been hurt. If you let it, the part that's been missing can be filled. It is our choices that lead us to our fates."

Nexhan didn't entirely understand everything Bessa had said, but her words dug up something deep inside him.

She looked behind her then said, biting her lip, "You should go now. And a little word of advice? Begging on your knees might earn you some points." She winked then returned to her stones, ignoring him completely and whispering things to herself.

Begging. On his knees. He could probably do that. *Should,* he amended. He got up and vanished into the forest in search of Cole. She hadn't actually said where he could find him, but something told Nexhan he was in the right place.

* * * *

Cole sighed as he picked at the bark of an oak. Everyone's excitement with the upcoming mating was driving him insane. Geez, was this what he would have to go through? *Big* if *there, buddy.* He felt sorry for the male who was about to commit himself, but the dude was all silly smiles. Well, Cole guessed when in love, stupidity was excusable. *Whatever.*

He knew he was just being grumpy and he hated that a part of him was jealous. It was weird, after running for so long from Bessa and the pressure to mate her that he now craved all the flowers and food and decorations... Of course, that wasn't going to happen. He had allowed himself to entertain fantasies of him and Nexhan vowing themselves to each other with his family around him.

Cole growled and tossed the thought away. He wasn't going to think about 'what ifs' and 'could haves'. It was a waste of time and brainpower. He needed to decide what he wanted to do with his life. When he and Kale had arrived after their journey, Cole had gone straight to his parents and told them the truth. He had been a bit stunned when his father crushed him into a big bear hug and told him how much he loved him. Of course, Kale being Kale, had to rub in the point that he'd 'told him so'. A weight had lifted from Cole's shoulders then. And he'd made good with Bessa, who was happy to have him back and was adamant that she didn't hold anything against him for stringing her along.

Things couldn't have been better.

Yeah, right. He was still hurting and he hated it. Everything had ended so badly between him and Nexhan. *Maybe it's better this way. Clean separation.* What had he honestly expected? They were from different clans. And now that Cole thought about it, Nexhan's *big idea* made sense.

Still, he missed the male desperately.

Cole leaned against the tree and hung his head low, trying to forget the way Nexhan felt against him—all that heat and hardness and hair like the midnight sky—and the times they'd shared just lounging on the forest floor, holding one another. Cole recalled something he'd heard in the city. *'You always remember your first love.'*

Fan-fucking-tastic. Are first loves supposed to hurt this much?

"How the hell am I supposed to forget you?" he whispered to himself.

"I don't want you to."

Cole snapped his head up and frowned. He was hallucinating—he had to be. Maybe he was dreaming? Nexhan stood before him looking delicious and—serious. Cole blinked for a moment. "What. The. Fuck."

Nexhan smiled meekly. "Bessa told me I'd find you here. Lovely female."

Okay, maybe he wasn't dreaming, but why would Nexhan be here? "What... Ah..." With anger burning inside him, he snapped, "Why were you talking to her?"

Nexhan raised his hands in an appeasing gesture. "Your clan was curious to see how we were getting along and equally thrilled to have a Rune Fang as witness to the mating ceremony."

"Oh that," Cole scowled, hating to be reminded of all the bliss that he would never be able to sample. *Don't say that... I might meet someone... Pfft.* The idea of mating anyone else but Nexhan was strangely repulsive to him.

"I have to admit that when I first heard of this mating, my heart fell. I thought you had decided to unite with Bessa —"

Cole interrupted him. "What does it matter if I had? Why are you bothering me? In case you're too dense to notice, I'm here because I want to be alone."

Nexhan sighed wearily. "Cole, I know I've wronged you —"

"*Wronged*? Wronged!" He balled his fists and gnashed his teeth. He was of a mind to smash his knuckles into Nexhan's puss, but he knew he'd just end up hurting himself. "Is that what you call it? You made me feel more like a failure than I ever had before!" Tears pricked the corner of his eyes. He refused to shed a tear in front of the man, refused to let anyone ever again see that part of him.

Nexhan accepted his words stoically. "It was not my intention to hurt you, Cole. I was terrified that you would have been injured — or worse."

Cole huffed. "You have a funny of showing it. Besides, why should you anyway? You made it quite clear that I was nothing more than a fuck."

"That was a lie," Nexhan said softly and stepped forward.

Cole sensed that the man was agitated with Cole's flippant attitude, but he was making a huge effort to keep his tone polite. Cole didn't understand. He couldn't deal with this. He'd finally come to accept that there could be nothing between them and now the bastard was stirring up the hurt all over again? "What do you want from me?"

"Forgiveness," he said, those big yellow eyes sparkling.

When Cole just glared at him, Nexhan dropped to his knees and dipped his head.

"I come to apologize, to beg forgiveness."

Cole looked around, waiting for someone to come out and tell him this was all a big joke. This couldn't be real. He swallowed hard unsure how to react. He decided just to be straight with the male. "I trusted you. You led me to believe that you actually cared about me. Maybe I was just seeing things that weren't really there, but—damn it! You made me feel like shit! I'm *not* a cub! I am a *man*!"

"I know," Nexhan said simply. He knelt there motionless, waiting. "And I did care. I *do*."

Cole huffed. Could he forgive him? He'd never before felt so betrayed, so empty...

Nexhan looked up at him with lovely, shiny eyes. "There is no excuse for what I've done, but I do have an explanation."

This intrigued Cole. He didn't respond but leaned against a tree in acceptance and waited. He was actually enjoying the big lug on his knees. He looked so vulnerable.

"You want to know about Inari," he said shakily.

From Nexhan's earlier outburst, Cole knew that this was a touchy subject.

"We were... We were lovers for decades. We were supposed to have been mated, but he wouldn't let me bond with him in fear that our enemies might seek to hurt him in order to hurt me. At that time, things were...perilous."

Cole swallowed a lump as he listened to the male's shaky voice. He hadn't expected this.

Nexhan took a deep breath and continued. "One hundred years ago, we were betrayed by one of our own. My mother was slaughtered, my father died protecting the clan, my breed-mate was taken... The only way we survived was by taking refuge under *Weynka Le Gai*'s roots." Nexhan closed his eyes as his voice hitched. "Inari died in my arms. I couldn't save him. His wounds were too severe. Perhaps if we had been bonded... Donoma and his hawks came and together we pushed back the threat."

Cole's throat closed. A part of him wanted to throw Nexhan's pain back in his face just so he knew what Cole had felt like, but he couldn't do that. He cared about him too much. Unsure what to say or do, he just listened.

Nexhan shuddered. "I left my home in a quest for vengeance to slay those few who had escaped the aftermath and, for a long time, it consumed me. Even after I found it, I could not return. Too many memories, too much hurt..." Nexhan looked into Cole's eyes. "I had a dream one night. Inari was standing among the sequoias, his hands outstretched. Every time I'd try to reach for him, he'd get farther away. When I awoke, I knew I had to return. And then *you* happened," Nexhan turned angry, his brows pulling down. "I thought by loving you, I was betraying Inari. I was so sure Inari and I were true-mates."

Cole swallowed hard, focusing on choice words. Did he hear right? When Nexhan sniffed, Cole found himself moving toward the male. He dropped down in front of the Rune Fang and pulled him into a big hug. Nexhan accepted him easily, burying his face in the crook of Cole's neck.

"The pain is too much sometimes." His breath hitched. "But, when I'm with you...I feel free. Right."

Cole didn't say anything, just held the big male close. Understanding rolled through him. He couldn't comprehend the pain that Nexhan had experienced with losing his family, but losing the one he'd loved? Yeah. He got that now and maybe their fight needed to happen so he'd know what Nexhan had gone through. He wet his lips. "I forgive you."

He felt Nexhan's surprise. "Truly?"

"Yeah," Cole whispered. "I just wished you would have told me this sooner."

Nexhan looked at Cole, his eyes shimmering. "I loved Inari deeply. I still do. But, there is one thing I've learned," he said, placing Cole's palm against his heart. "There's room in here for you too."

Cole parted his lips to speak, but he failed to find the words. This all seemed like a dream, a desperate delusion cooked up by his mind to sooth his aching heart. He moved his mouth a few times before he finally asked, "What knocked you in the head?"

Nexhan smiled softly. "It took the berating of a very wise woman and a loyal friend to make me see the truth."

Frowning, Cole wasn't sure he understood. He had no idea what to do. Was Nexhan saying he wanted more from Cole? Did *he* even want more?

Nexhan saw his confusion and smiled ruefully. "There is another reason I'm here. I know what you are, Cole."

"R-really?" he stuttered.

"It took countless hours of searching, but Donoma and I discovered an old tome that the hawk had given to me for safe keeping when I was just a cub. I'd hidden it and hadn't thought to look at it until he remembered something mentioned in it. It detailed a very gifted eagle touched by the Mother, who walked in the shadow of the Father to battle the uprising Kaga that had ravaged the earth, before the fall of our greatest city."

"That old, huh?" Cole asked astonished and a bit anxious. *Get to the details!*

Nexhan grinned. "Coleban Nicoyla, I deem you Life-Binder."

"What? No confetti?" Cole pursed his lips and looked around.

Nexhan let loose a roar of laughter and pulled Cole close to him. He ruffled his hair roughly.

"Hey!" Cole bristled. When they finally settled, he asked, "So, what exactly does that mean?"

"It means that you are unique, Cole. Something so precious and amazing, words cannot describe," Nexhan took Cole's hand and ran his fingers lightly over his palm. "The ability to heal and return the soul to the body —"

Cole gaped. "Resurrection?"

Nexhan nodded. "Yes. With his tears, he cleansed the body of poison and the brother was new with life. Where he walked, moss grew and upon his blood, life sprang up." Something mischievous passed in Nexhan's eyes. "And upon his seed, flowers bloomed."

"That's so weird," Cole grumbled.

Nexhan gripped Cole's face in between his palms. "Your potential is limitless, Cole. After reading that book, everything made sense, everything connected. The bird, the grove... The Kaga. They fear you. They cannot touch you. They are death and you are life. Life negates death."

"Isn't it the other way around too?" Cole asked disbelievingly.

"Death is temporary. Life is free and wild and as long as there is a universe, the potential for life exists," Nexhan explained enthusiastically. "In time you will learn to bend life to *your* will."

"But how come I have such a problem communicating?" he whispered, still unable to come to terms with everything.

"I have a theory about that. Remember when you said that you feel like there was something caged inside of you? That you felt like it wanted to get out? I think that you've been holding back your true self for so long, it has created a sort of backlash, a static. I can't imagine all the energy you have got up in this little hot body. Your nature is to heal, to create life. That's why you couldn't harm that deer and it's why you're unable to hunt successfully. It goes against your nature."

Everything seemed to hit Cole at once. He could do all that stuff? *Well, duh?* The incident with the raccoon and the bird made sense now. The grove—*damn it.* He didn't want to be special. All his life he just wanted to be adequate.

He backed away and got up, snarling, "Well, I don't want it!"

"It's not a choice, Cole," Nexhan said, beleaguered.

"Sure it is. I choose not to use it," he barked.

"That's like saying the sun won't rise. It's inevitable, natural," Nexhan reasoned.

"I'm nothing special," Cole went on.

"It is not for us to know the way of the gods," he said sadly. "Many a time I've asked myself why Inari was taken from me—screamed it to the heavens, demanding an answer. I can only trust that they had a reason and they know what they are doing."

Cole stayed silent as he studied the ground. He swallowed hard, the back of his throat burning. Why him? He was nothing special. There were other candidates out there more worthy than him. Why had the Mother chosen him? And what was he going to do with this supposed gift? Go around touching people to heal their hangnails?

Nexhan covered Cole in a soothing embrace. He whispered in Cole's ear, "It's okay. I'll do this with you. We'll figure it out together."

Together. As in…? He shifted around and looked into Nexhan's gorgeous eyes. They were so deep, so full of…*love?* Dare he hope? Nexhan cupped his cheek and ran his thumb over Cole's lips and he knew it was all over. He wasn't sure who moved first, but he balled his fist in the male's hair as Cole fed at his mouth with eager lips and their tongues clashed. Cole couldn't help but fight for control of the kiss, still wanting to punish Nexhan for the hurt he'd caused.

"There is one thing you must know, Cole," Nexhan breathed heavily. "I can't survive another loss. When you die, I want to go with you, forever joined. Bind yourself to me."

That should scare him more than it did, but deep down, Cole realized that that was what he wanted—a true-mate, someone to share himself with. And should he die, he wanted to make the journey alongside the one he loved.

"Don't expect to be bossing me around with your macho, I-am-clan-leader-and-you-will-obey-me routine," Cole admonished "That isn't going to fly with me anymore. Got it?"

Nexhan grinned fiercely and returned to kissing Cole until he was breathless. Somehow they'd ended up on the ground in a tangle of limbs, Nexhan's rough hands clawing at his shirt. They were naked in the flap of a hawk's wings.

"Wait, what do we do?" Cole sputtered. *Stupid question.* Of course, all shifters instinctively knew how it worked, but… He trembled.

"It's okay," Nex whispered.

Cole felt better when he recognized Nexhan's own fear. It was good to know he wasn't the only one scared shitless by the prospect of binding their souls.

Nexhan made a move as if he were going kiss him again. Instead, he moved lower and seductively sucked Cole's nipple into his mouth. Cole arched his back and groaned. *Yeah, that feels good.* So nice to experience a familiar touch again. Exploratory fingers probed at his ass. Mmm, what they needed was—

A drop of amber goo smacked him on the forehead. "Hey, just what I was thinking. I might be able to get used to this hocus-pocus."

Nexhan chuckled and collected a handful of sap from a tree. He gently smeared it across Cole's ass, making sure to circle his rim enticingly. When Cole was mush in his hands, Nexhan said, "This won't be easy, Cole. There will be people, magical and shifter alike, who will want to exploit your gifts. But I swear to you that I'll always be there to protect you."

Nodding, Cole pulled Nexhan to him for a tender kiss. "You got to help me through this. I don't know why I was chosen, but it scares the crap out of me."

Nexhan answered by sliding himself into Cole. He gasped at the intrusion then sighed contently. How he'd missed this feeling, the warmth and fullness – it was divine. Nexhan let Cole adjust to his size then slowly retreated until he nearly slipped out only to dive back in deep. Cole groaned and clawed at his lover's shoulders.

Running his fingers through Cole's short locks, Nexhan asked, "Do you want me to go first?"

Cole swallowed hard and nodded. He was terrified, but he knew why Nexhan had made the offer. Nexhan had wronged him, no matter how they looked at it or tried to excuse it, he had. By offering to go first, Nexhan was trusting Cole with his very soul and that was the dealmaker. Cole knew he could do this. He wanted this. Nexhan was *his*.

He had expected a sharp pain, but what he got was a warm, soft lick. He moaned and turned his head to the side, giving the male more room to work. Something inside him tumbled, making his stomach hurt. *Just relax.* Nexhan's breath glided over Cole's skin. He closed his eyes and concentrated on his lover's heartbeat, the feel of the man's cock inside him. Cole's heart skipped a beat when Nexhan whispered "*I love you*" right before pain pieced his skin. Cole groaned against the bite and wrapped his legs around Nexhan's hips, locking his ankles.

Nexhan sucked. The pain melted away and pleasured bloomed in Cole. Nexhan made a small noise against Cole's neck and Cole glanced at the exposed skin of his lover's shoulder. He licked his lips, his fangs coming down. All he had to do was bite and suck then they'd be bound for eternity. That was what he wanted. He felt Nexhan's fear that Cole might change his mind and not complete the ritual so he said, "*I love you*" too, playfully adding a reference to the man's size then plunged in.

He sank his fangs into Nexhan's flesh easily, as if he were biting into butter. The man moaned and at the first taste of Nexhan's exquisite blood, an excruciating pain jolted through him. Instead of retreating, he hugged Nexhan closer, digging his fingers onto the male's back while Nexhan balled his fist in Cole's hair. They groaned in unison, both trying to beat back this unexpected turn of events. It felt as if his soul was being ripped apart.

He supposed that was what was really happening. It was only a moment of unbearable agony before an immense warmth flowed through him. Cole saw things... Things long passed and recently experienced...

A beautiful woman who smiled at him as a mother does to a child...

A sister sticking her tongue out in play...

A light-haired male who told him he'd always be with him...

The fight to survive against cruel enemies...

Cole saw himself as he lazed in the new growth...

The flash of white robes...

Memories. Nexhan's memories. So many. So joyous. So sad. Cole could feel Nexhan's love for him. He could feel... *Him*...

He couldn't believe what was happening. He thought he was going to die from the overload and just when he thought he couldn't take anymore, they erupted into an orgasm simultaneously. They groaned against each other's necks as Cole came all over his stomach and Nexhan spurted deep inside him. Surely, he must already be dead, for nothing this heavenly could be earthly.

Cole wasn't sure when he came back down, but he awoke to Nexhan stroking his cheek. Cole sighed and opened his eyes, feeling strange things. Something very primal and powerful was running through him, lighting him up. His lips twitched in a smile, "Hey, big boy."

"How do you feel?" Nexhan asked sleepily.

"I feel...good. I feel...things... I can feel you as if I am you, but I'm me. It's weird, I can't explain it," he said huskily.

"I know what you mean." Nexhan grinned.

"We're bound now." It was a statement. Cole could feel a part of Nexhan inside him, and it was amazing.

Nexhan nodded and kissed him softly on the lips. "It's astonishing what you have inside of you, Cole. So pure, so wonderful and beautiful it makes me want to cry."

"No crying," Cole muttered and pushed an errant lock behind Nexhan's ear. "Can I ask you something?"

"Yes, you can have whatever you want." Nexhan beamed happily.

Cole stuck his bottom lip out for a moment. *Guess that's the price of being bonded.* "I was going to say you don't even know what I was going to ask, but I guess you do, so humor me."

Chuckling, Nexhan said, "Okay. Ask away."

"I want a ceremony — with flowers and lots of food and lots of stupid cute things that make you want to puke, and my family and your clan and the hawks... I want it *all*. Not now... Maybe later. Can I have it?" he asked, looking into his lover's eyes. Somehow, Nexhan had developed green streaks in his left eye.

Nexhan boomed with laughter and delight. "Yes, I'll give it to you. Stupidly cute decorations and all."

Cole sighed as they embraced. The first stirrings of arousal hit them both at the same time, probably down to the nanosecond, he guessed. That was part of the bond—the ability to share in one's emotions and desires. He'd never before felt closer to anyone and for the first time in his life, he was content—happy. He knew it wouldn't be easy. Like all couples, they'd have their arguments and disagreements, but in the end, they had each other. Cole wasn't sure where this whole Life-Binder thing would take him, but only one thing mattered.

Nexhan would be there every step of the way.

Somewhere in the distance, Cole thought he heard a crow caw.

Glossary of Terms

Akumai'ai — A legendary bow imbued with magic. It was created by the wolf-shifters from the trees of Shairobi and gifted to the Rune Fangs.

Anunaki — Sumerian gods.

Callari — One of the Three.

The Coming — The time when the shifters left their home world and arrived on earth over thirty-thousand years ago.

Cougar-shifter — Also known as Guardians.

Darkness — The entity that governs the negative energies in the universe.

Eagle-shifter — Also known as the Messengers.

Earth-speak — A way of communication using the energies flowing from out off the earth while in animal form.

Earth-Touched — Those gifted with the sight of precognition.

Empath — Those gifted with the ability to sense and manipulate emotions.

The Gray Man — One of the Three.

Hawk-shifter — Also known as the lords of air.

Kaga — Demons and the shifters' archenemies, created by Darkness to steal their magic.

Life-Binder — Those blessed with an incredibly rare gift of healing and in some cases, resurrection.

Loupen — Peaceful clan of werewolves.

Lycan—Cousins to the Loupen, but bigger, stronger with an insatiable appetite for death.

Mother Goddess—The divine being that governs all life.

Mi'wisa—Term of respect often afford to high ranking members, usually the clan leader.

Oketa—A crow or raven in the service of the Gray Man.

Qui'nodo'nai—Language that was spoken in Shairobi. All shifter dialects are based on this tongue.

Rune Fang—Saber-toothed-like cats. Also known as the Gatekeepers.

Shairobi—The shifter's home world.

Shaman—Those gifted with the ability to control the elements. Many have the ability to heal.

The Three—A group of three mysterious god-like beings.

True-Mates—Those destined from creation to unite. True-Mates will be reborn continuously until they find each other in life and bond their souls.

Weynka Le Gai—The giant sequoia that is the source of the Rune Fang's magic.

Weywoni Le Gai—The redwood forest in which the Rune Fangs make their home. Also known as Redwood National Park in California.

Wolf-shifter—Also known as Fenrir or the Hunters. They are extinct.

About the Author

Lupa Garneau is a romance and erotica author in both the gay and straight genres. She lives in Chicago—home of the best music scene on the planet!—with her Doberman Danni, and mew, Ollie.

Lupa Garneau loves to hear from readers. You can find her contact information, website details and author profile page at http://www.totallybound.com.

Totally Bound Publishing